Tropical Moonlight

Book Three

Tropical Breeze Series

Michele Gilcrest

Chapter 1

Frankie

"Excuse me, coming through. Hi, excuse me. Running late. Sorry, coming through," Frankie Jones bellowed while juggling her luggage in one hand and cell phone in the other. She'd just landed from a week's stay with her boyfriend, Christian, in Atlanta. It was their second trip of the year. While maintaining a long-distance relationship had come with its challenges, they'd proven they were determined to see what would come of it.

For now, it was back to island life, and the first thing on Frankie's agenda was stopping by the office at the resort.

"Christian, are you still there?" she asked while trying to regain her normal breathing rhythm.

"I'm here. Just thinking how nice it would be to

turn back the clock. Imagine an extra day to tune everything out and just hang out together. Just the two of us." He sighed, then continued. "Instead, it's back to the grind here at headquarters. As we speak, I'm waiting for the boss to conjure up my next assignment."

Hustling down a long corridor and shifting her way past other passengers was Frankie's strong suit. In the hospitality field, she'd only done it a thousand times.

As she arrived at the conveyor belt, she dropped her carry-on bag to the floor, patiently waiting for her things. "I know. Lately it seems like our visits can't come soon enough. But hey, it comes along with the territory of dating long distance. Besides, we've got this, right? Give it another three or four months and we'll be back together again, planning our next adventure."

The sound of Christian's chuckle made her smile. "And, in between visits there's always video calls," he said.

In the background, the baggage siren she'd been waiting for alerted the crowd. With a quick glance at her watch, Frankie calculated ten minutes to find her transportation, and another fifteen to arrive at The Cove. "Yes, speaking of video calls, how about we make a date for this evening? Are you free around seven?"

"Seven works. After a long first day back it's

likely I'll want to kick up my feet and indulge in some take out while we talk."

She giggled. "I bet you'd order take out every day of the week if it were feasible."

"You might be on to something."

Frankie shook her head as if he could see her. "I know I am," she replied. Then her smile dissipated. "Listen, I have to run. My luggage just hit the belt. I'll shoot you a text once I arrive at the resort."

"Sounds good."

As she bobbed and weaved her head around a few shoulders, Frankie spotted her three additional bags. The smallest piece was for toiletries and hair products. The next in size carried all of her shoes, and the last bag included all of her clothing, carefully folded and lined with plastic bags from the cleaners. It was a trick she'd learned years ago that kept the wrinkles away every time.

Why do I always pack like I'm leaving the country for a year? She groaned.

Nestled in her hand was the muffled sound of Christian's voice calling from her cell phone. "Frankie? ... Frankie?" she heard.

"Yes, sorry, I'm still here. I'm trying not to lose track of the luggage."

"No problem, I'll let you go," he said.

Following a brief moment Christian's voice echoed, "Frankie."

"Yes?" she said, replying with very little focus.

"I love you."

The feeling of a growing lump in the most inconvenient location of her throat blocked her vocals. Or at least it felt like it. She struggled. Not because anything was particularly wrong. She just couldn't quite say the words back. Feeling frozen in time, Frankie watched as the world revolved around her. Then it hit her. "Christian, are you there?" she asked.

Now, let's face it. She knew that pretending as if the line was muffled with static was wrong. But what else could she say?

Why does this feel so awkward? she wondered.

A friendly gentleman standing in front of her pointed. "Do those bags belong to you?"

In the background she heard Christian saying, "Go get your luggage. We'll talk soon."

"Okay," she answered, then disconnected the line.

After offering somewhat of a dumbfounded stare, Frankie responded to the man, "Yes, thank you. The three red bags belong to me. If you wouldn't mind putting them right here, that would be wonderful."

"No problem," he said, stacking quickly without breaking a sweat. "How's that?"

"Perfect, thank you. All I have to do is lean and roll from here," she said, as she demonstrated with a swift movement of the hand.

"You sure?"

"I'm positive." She smiled. "I'm a natural born pro at this point, but thanks again for your help."

"Okay, you take care now." Following a head nod, the kind stranger disappeared.

With a huge thrust forward, Frankie rolled through the automatic doors, immediately consumed by the warmth of the Bahamas breeze. There was no other place that gave her such a warm welcome. If she were being honest, there was no other place she'd call home.

In the distance she saw several shuttles lined up, each labeled with names of various hotels. The shuttle for The Cove was white with gold cursive writing. She'd only seen it a thousand times as she watched guests arrive and leave the resort. Then there was her personal usage of the service whenever she visited Christian. Speaking of Christian. How in the world was she going to explain her little mishap if he'd noticed? *Did he notice?* she wondered. She could barely make sense of it herself. She cared for him a lot. But love? *Are we really ready for love?* she questioned.

In effort to gain traction, Frankie adjusted the bag on her shoulder, along with her purse. Then, with a quick swivel-like motion she began shifting herself to pull the rolling load instead of pushing. Unfortunately, in true miscalculated fashion, the entire stack toppled over, leaving her frustrated.

Frankie closed her eyes, and chose to count backwards. It was supposed to be a calming technique in moments like these. Although, it didn't always work for her.

Breathe, she whispered.

While reaching for her bags, the rugged sound of a male voice spoke from behind, reverberating through her body. "Well, well, well," he spoke.

The voice felt so familiar. But in a pure moment of haste, Frankie swung around and fired back, "Well, what?"

That's when a feeling of lightheadedness washed over her. In Frankie's mind, this day wasn't real. It couldn't be. Because if it were real, she wouldn't be standing face-to-face with David Sullivan. Maybe some other man. But David? Resurrected from a previous chapter in her life that was supposed to be closed forever? Him? No way.

Standing six-feet tall, with a low-cut beard, and meticulously trimmed sideburns, was none other than David in the flesh. A man she'd never spoken about to anyone.

"Looks like you could use some help." He smiled.

Frankie held her hand out. "I'm fine."

Simultaneously, they plunged toward the same bag, accidentally knocking into each other.

She clenched her teeth. "It's fine, really. You don't have to —"

Frankie watched as he proceeded to ignore her and organize the bags just the same.

He adjusted the shades on his head and chuckled. "I see some things haven't changed. It's okay to accept a little help every now and again, ya know."

Unsure of what to do she motioned toward the bags. "This really isn't necessary, David."

The awkward moment nearly distracted her from looking for her shuttle. But when she did look up, she noticed the rear end of her bus departing several feet away.

"Great. Jussst great," she said, allowing her hand to slap down on her thigh.

"What? Do you want me to stack them differently?" he asked.

"No, the bags are fine." She relaxed. "I was referring to my ride — the shuttle bus to the resort. It just pulled out of the space leaving me with another fifteen minutes to kill before the next one arrives."

She noticed him smiling the same intoxicating smile that almost caused her to give up everything. The same smile that made her want to have his baby years ago. Unfortunately, almost becoming a Sullivan was something she had to bury in her history of heartaches, never to be spoken of again.

"I'd offer you a ride, but I'm actually catching a shuttle myself," he explained.

She stood quietly thinking, *It's not like I would get in the car with you anyway.*

As Frankie noticed his hand still resting comfortably on her bags he spoke up. "It's been a long time. How have you been?"

She flashed back, imagining their last moments together. Like it was yesterday, she saw them standing in front of a ticket booth in the center of Grand Central Station. It was one of the busiest days of the year, Christmas Eve. It was also the last place she wore her engagement ring, prior to slipping it off and placing it in the palm of his hand.

"Frankie."

In a disoriented fashion, she responded, "Yeah, um, I've been good. Great, actually. How about yourself?"

He wavered, glancing over at the passing traffic. "Busy, as usual. Probably too busy for my own good, but the bills have to get paid somehow, right?"

"Yeah, you were always on the go. But as you said, I guess some things don't change," she said, trying not to notice his fit physique, bare ring finger, and overall, well-groomed appearance. Especially since she was a sucker for a well-groomed man with just the right touch of ruggedness about him.

"Touché," he responded.

Frankie took a step toward her luggage. "Well, it was nice seeing you, but I really better get going. Long day ahead. Thanks again for your help."

As he stepped back, she grabbed hold of the handles, strategically maneuvering so as not to have a second mishap.

"That's it?" he called out.

Frankie pointed toward the shuttles. "I have to get to work."

David shrugged his shoulders. "Okay. One would just think you'd be a little curious after all these years, maybe even a few questions lingering through your mind about how life turned out. And, since it's rare that we'd get an opportunity to see each other — I don't know, I just find it odd that you'd want to walk away."

Frankie contemplated whether to ignore the comment or to turn around and tell him off like she should've done years ago in Grand Central. The latter wasn't really an option, but it still crossed her mind. Going against her better judgment she took the bait. "What kind of questions would you expect me to have after all these years, David? Especially after the way things ended. How your life turned out is your business, not mine."

He tilted his head slightly. "I wondered those things about you. Do you have any idea how long I waited for you to come back that day? I waited for you to reach out, call me back, show up at my door, write a letter. Heck, I would've even accepted an old-fashioned telegram if it meant I could hear from you. That was the worst year of my life, Frankie. The worst Christmas, worst everything one could possibly imagine. And, I always promised myself if I ever saw you again, the least I would do is ask why."

Wow, was the only thing that came to mind as she stood with her eyes widened. The audacity. After all, he was the one who set the dominoes in motion that led towards their breakup, not her. The only thing she was responsible for was doing the inevitable by breaking things off before he did.

Luckily, another shuttle to The Cove was in sight, arriving earlier than expected. This time she wasn't missing it.

She cleared her throat. "Again, David, I can't thank you enough for your help today, and it was certainly a surprise running into you, but —"

He nodded. "I get it. You have to go. Again."

"Right."

With no mention of what transpired between the two, or how it made her feel, Frankie pressed onward, moving toward her shuttle. Besides, what was she supposed to feel emotionally after all these years? David was someone she fell in love with for the brief year she lived with her cousin in New York. In hindsight, she was lucky things turned out the way they did. New York turned out to be a pit stop, but not a place she could permanently call home. She wasn't supposed to fall in love. At least not back then she wasn't. With her track record, sometimes she questioned if she was ever supposed to fall in love.

After surrendering her bags to the driver, Frankie hoisted herself up the steps of the shuttle. When she landed at the top, the sound of the same familiar voice was just a few feet away.

With an eye roll she turned back giving a look that spoke volumes.

David held up his itinerary, flashing it while stepping toward the doorway. "I'm not following you if that's what you're thinking. I have a reservation just like everyone else on this shuttle."

"Mmm," she grunted.

He paused, standing close enough for her to feel his breath. "Don't worry, I'm sure The Cove has more than enough property to accommodate the two of us without me getting in your way."

Frankie clenched as he inched around her searching for a seat. What he didn't know was The Cove was her place of business, and she would do everything to ensure he didn't find out.

Chapter 2

Meg

With the sound of the waves crashing, Meg marveled at the crystal-clear view of the water. Cleaning windows in the Oceanside suite wasn't exactly her favorite way to help keep the B&B running. But while Parker was still interviewing for staff, she vowed to help fill in the gaps wherever needed.

Inhaling the ocean breeze brought back memories of her days, not long ago, of working at the resort. It was around this time, midday, she'd steal away if she could, strolling by the private beach, dreaming of ways to actually run a resort someday. And, while she hadn't quite invested in a business of her own, she'd fallen for and joined careers with a man who was pushing her in the right direction. Some would say it was a potentially risky move for a couple that wasn't married yet, but she was learning the ropes of the business with Parker, the man she planned to spend forever with.

As the memories continued running through her mind she felt a pair of hands slip around her waist.

"You've been working since the minute you arrived this morning. Surely, there's a law against such behavior," Parker said, stealing a kiss from her neck.

Meg swatted a towel at him, discouraging all forms of fraternizing while the guests were up and about. "Parker," she whispered. "You need to behave yourself. Mr. Barnes is right next door in the Ocean Pearl suite, we have other guests down the hall, and our new arrivals should be here any minute now."

She felt his fingers kneading into her shoulders as he said, "I know, but that still doesn't stop me from wanting to steal away with you. Even if only for a minute."

Who was she kidding? she thought. Meg loved stealing away just as much as he did. And, when she pretended to resist, he knew she was only flirting with him.

Cracking a smile, she responded, "Do you remember how much we longed for these moments when I worked at The Cove?"

Parker nodded. "Do I? That was back in the days when I tried to show up and surprise you with lunch, unknowingly stirring up trouble with your cranky boss. Former boss, that is."

"Yep, she was quite a handful. Word around the island is that she's still as miserable as ever," Meg said. "But thankfully, that's no longer a concern of mine."

"Is that the word around the island, or the word from your best friend and roomie, Frankie?"

Grinning, she said. "Maybe a little of both." She watched as Parker grabbed the hand towel and her caddy in one hand, and extended his other hand toward her.

"Follow me," he beckoned.

"Parker, you're joking, right? I still have to finish the windows. Didn't you hear the part where I said the guests will be arriving soon?"

"I heard everything you said. Don't worry, we have everything under control. The windows look perfect. And, I love the new signs on all the suites with the beachy names — nice touch. The guests will love it." He winked.

Meg placed her hand in his, happy that he'd noticed and was pleased with everything.

Parker stopped to look into her eyes. "Having you here with me and watching you add your special touch is exactly what the B&B needed. It's what I needed. I know we get so busy here at times, still needing more staff, still needing to finish the second portion of the B&B, and dealing with one thing or the other — including taking care of Mr. Barnes. But, just in case I don't say it enough, I'm grateful to have you as my manager."

Meg agreed with his assessment of everything. They had been off to a busy start, building their reputation at the B&B and still housing the man, affectionately known as Old Man Barnes. Even as his strength was continuing to decline. Parker had a soft spot in his heart, knowing he'd eventually have to either stay with his estranged son, which was highly unlikely, or check into a nursing home.

Meg inhaled. "You literally have five-minutes and not a minute more. Where are you taking me?"

"You'll see when you get there. Trust me."

She followed him down two flights of stairs, and found herself in a basement with old boxes, cobwebs, and a wooden chest.

Meg paused. "Yeah, I'm not much of a basement kind of gal. The cobwebs alone are enough to give me the creeps."

"I know. That's why I've been down here working feverishly to sort through things and create some sort of order. But I found something today that I thought may be of interest. Something you may be able to add your creative touch to," he replied.

"What is it?"

A few feet away, Parker tugged on a large wooden frame with an old photo of a couple. As she grew closer, it was evident the picture included Barnes.

Meg ran her hands along the trim, marveling at its beauty, then stood back. "Is that his wife, Evelyn?"

"I believe it is. Their names are on the back. They look so good together. So happy."

"They look like they're so in love. And, she's such a beautiful woman. I can only imagine how heartbroken he must've been when she passed away. Did he ever reveal the cause of death?" Meg asked.

"No, and I couldn't find the nerve to ask. He already seems so riddled with pain. I didn't want to expose an old wound."

"Makes sense," she spoke. She then grabbed her towel and dusted the frame.

Parker continued. "I don't know if you remember this, but the night we discovered old photos at the beach house, you came up with a fantastic idea. One that we never fully had the chance to implement."

Meg squinted. "What was that?"

"You said that I should incorporate some of the elements of the old beach house and the owner's style into the renovations, remember?"

"Yes, I almost forgot," she replied, exposing her dimples.

"Well, we did the best we could to give it that beachy feel, incorporated with the fresh designs and whatnot, but this time I really see this as an opportunity that shouldn't be missed. It's special," he explained. "I was thinking we should incorporate this picture of the original owners, somewhere on the main floor. This way the guests can enjoy a little history. Maybe we could even get a plaque made up to explain their story and their contributions to the B&B. We could hang it right below the frame. What do you think?"

"Now that, Parker Wilson, is a genius idea. It will add a personal touch, tying in a little of the old with the new. Who doesn't love a little history? Especially the history of a B&B and the love story of its original owners," she squealed.

"Yes, that's exactly where I'm going with this. I figured you'd like the idea. We just need to run it by Barnes and make sure he's okay with it. I'd hate for him to discover this hanging up without his approval."

Meg raised a finger. "Agreed, but how about we ask on a day when he's in a good mood. You know everything as of late, depends on how he feels."

"Of course," Parker replied.

Meg envisioned a new driftwood or beach themed frame when their moment was interrupted by heels clanking down the stairs. "Hello? Is anybody down there?" a female voice called out.

Meg noticed long, tanned legs, with toes covered in fresh polish, a gold ring on one toe, and fancy sandals descending. The woman had a purse in one hand and a cherry blossom fan in the other.

Parker quickly placed the frame down and met

her at the stairwell. "Yes, welcome to Seaside B&B. How may we help you?"

Meg followed suit, offering a warm smile.

The woman's eyes scanned the basement as she fanned herself. She gave Meg the once over, then diverted most of her attention back to Parker.

"I'm Portia Fennley. I have a reservation for the Oceanside suite, and after a long day of travel, the last thing I feel like doing is standing around waiting for good customer service."

Parker nodded. "Yes, ma'am. Our apologies. We were just down here digging around. My name is Parker Wilson, owner of the B&B, and this is my manager, Meg."

Ms. Fennley flashed a half-hearted smile, then turned about face. "I have bags in the main lobby, Parker. If you wouldn't mind—"

Meg watched as Parker hurried along to accommodate her. If this woman's manners weren't properly checked at the front door, she and Parker were definitely in for an interesting week.

In the main lobby, Meg slipped behind the computer at the front desk. After a few clicks she said, "The reservation shows that Mr. Fennley will be joining you in the Oceanside suite. Is he on his way?"

The woman moaned. "About that." She then slapped a credit card on the desk with his name on it. "We agreed it would be best for him to have his own room. He'll be in shortly. He's outside grabbing the rest of our things."

Meg hesitated. "Okay. Well, we do have the Seabreeze suite available, but are you certain that's what you want to do? I'd hate for you to incur the additional expense."

Mrs. Fennley stopped glancing at Parker long enough to throw a dagger her way. If looks could kill, Meg would certainly be in a heap of trouble.

"Sweetheart, thank you for your concern, but the money is not an issue," Mrs. Fennley explained. She then waved her fan toward the computer. "Now, if you'll just go ahead and make the arrangements, I can get settled in my room. Perhaps, Parker would be willing to escort me."

Meg encouraged herself to keep a straight face. *Who does this woman think she is?* she thought.

Let's face it, Meg was used to the hospitality industry, and knew how important it was to be professional. She'd experienced all the personality types, from the friendliest to the most high and mighty. The customer is always right had typically been her motto. But this woman's demeanor had an extra layer of sauce to it — an extra dose of something that didn't sit well with Meg. But, before she could gather her thoughts, Parker, who seemed oblivious to it all, was already leading Portia Fennley away.

At the front door, a gentleman entered, glistening with sweat and bogged down with more bags.

"Welcome to Seaside B&B. How may I help you?" Meg smiled.

"Hi, I'm Frank Fennley," he said, glancing up. "My wife came in ahead of me. Her name is —"

"Yes, Mr. Fennley. I have all your information right here. I'm Meg, it's nice to meet you."

"Likewise."

She tried not to stare, but Mr. Fennley looked nothing like she expected. She was looking for a man that was tall with swag, and maybe even with looks to kill to come walking through the door. Maybe she was looking for him to be the Ken, standing alongside his Barbie. But the man who stood in front of her was nothing like him.

If her guess was right, Portia Fennley was around thirty, thirty-five max. Mr. Fennley, on the other hand, looked more like her grandfather rather than her husband — not that it mattered, but it did catch her off guard.

He continued, divulging a lot more than Meg had asked for. "I overheard her from the front. Typically, I'd be embarrassed by the whole room separation thing, but this isn't the first time we've had a couples spat, causing us to sleep apart. I guess I still have a lot to learn about how to be a good husband to Mrs. Portia Fennley."

Not knowing what to say, Meg spoke on a whim. "Aww, I'm sure everything will be just fine after you have a chance to settle in here at the B&B. There's something about the ocean that has a way of relaxing you, and melting all your troubles away."

He glanced over at the view. "Is that so? Well, I hope it has the ability to work miracles. If not, I may end up leaving here a single man — not something I anticipated after only being married a year."

Meg swallowed, quietly wondering what could cause newlyweds to already be at extreme odds, especially in tropical paradise. Either way, it was obvious this couple was in need of way more than good hospitality.

Chapter 3

Frankie and Meg

Frankie found herself reading the lips of the people muted on the big screen as Christian spoke on the other end of the line. It had already been a long day, therefore settling for a brief telephone call sounded way more appealing than getting all dolled up for a live video date.

She kicked up her feet and nestled into the cushion while eating her favorite food.

"We need to talk," Christian said.

Frankie's mind wandered from the flat screen to the tasty new sauce Terry included with her order. It was all the buzz at the food stand earlier, and now she knew why.

"Frankie, are you still there?" Christian asked.

"Mmm, yes. Sorry, I'm here. I just got carried away by this new sauce Terry made. I'm telling you; the woman is talented. She really needs to think about opening her own restaurant. We go back and forth about it all the time. I mean, I can see why she doesn't want to deal with the overhead of having a brick and mortar, but still. Can you imagine the kind of business she'd bring in?"

"Yes, Terry is definitely talented, there's no doubt about it. But I was wondering if you heard what I was saying earlier?"

While licking her fingertips she said, "About what?"

"About us."

Frankie placed her fork on her plate, setting aside her ferocious appetite for seafood. "Okayyy. What about us?"

Frankie could only speculate this had something to do with their call earlier. And, if it did, could she really blame him for seeking an explanation? The man had confessed his true feelings for her only to be met with silence.

He continued. "Maybe I'm making too much of it, I'm not sure. But something seemed different with you during our last visit, Frankie. It's like you were preoccupied or something. It felt like you were here physically but mentally elsewhere."

She knocked over her soda in haste. "Crap."

"So, I'm right," he said.

"No, I just saturated myself and the entire

loveseat in orange soda — not paying attention to what I was doing, that's all," she grumbled.

"Do you need time to go clean things up?"

"No, I can grab a dish towel while we talk. Regarding what you said, I'm not sure what made you feel that way. I was under the impression we had a good week," she replied.

"We did at times. But I don't know how to describe it. It's almost as if there was an elephant in the room that nobody was willing to address. It was just different, that's all."

She looked at the phone. "But just this morning you were dreaming about our next get together."

Christian stumbled at first, but then became clear. "I'm not the one with the issue. Everything is good on my end and I honestly thought you felt the same way up until this recent trip. It's almost as if something is bothering you but you won't admit it. Whatever it is, I just want you to know you can feel comfortable talking to me, that's all."

Frankie dabbed her clothing, then ran warm water into a bucket. While searching for a solution to remove the stain she confessed, "Christian, I hadn't thought much of it, to be honest. If anything, I think we're tired and perhaps just need some rest."

"Come on, Frankie. That's a cop out and you know it."

She unscrewed the bottle cap, dumping way more of the solution in the bucket than needed. She really hadn't been thinking about their relationship much. Instead, Frankie was just living in the moment. In her eyes it was fun but still way too soon to weigh in with thoughts of love.

After listening to him biting into his food, Christian said, "I was hoping you'd speak to what happened earlier today. Specifically, the moment right after I told you I love you. It's fine with me if you don't feel the same, but I'd rather talk about it than just pretend like I didn't say it."

And, there it was. It was all the confirmation Frankie needed. He was onto her, detecting her lame attempt to avoid his confession of love. The truth is, she really did like Christian a lot. He'd been such a gentleman, coming to her aid the day they got stuck in the elevator, and looking out for her ever since. But love? She wasn't there yet. As a matter of fact, she didn't know if she'd ever get there with Christian.

"Christian, with every visit we have together, it gives us an opportunity to grow closer. It truly does get sweeter every time. However, we both know long-distance relationships can be challenging. I don't see anything wrong with taking our time. Wouldn't you agree?" she asked.

Immediately, she began feeling better knowing her response wasn't a cop out. Instead, it was a very wise and cautious approach.

"Of course, I see value in spending quality time. But you hadn't been talking like this beforehand.

You've never used the word challenging to describe what we have," he said.

"Well, if I were you, I wouldn't take it to heart. You know my history, Christian. I've had my share of heartache — not that you're to blame for any of it. But I just want to take our time and make sure this is right for both of us."

"Understood."

Frankie heard the words but knew deep down his ego was bruised. What was she to do? How was a woman in her mid-forties who'd experienced one breakup after the other supposed to figure out this thing called love. She couldn't exactly use her parents as an example. They'd had their failed attempts at it over and over again.

Frankie's memories of her parent's relationship was something she knew she never wanted for herself. There were always the late-night work shifts for her dad. At least that's what he called it. And, the long arguments with mom whenever he finally returned home. All the tension, the slammed doors, the make-ups to breakups. Frankie remembered it all too well and wanted no part of it.

Then there were her own failed attempts at love. She could list them one-by-one. She could easily recall all the liars, the cheats, and even the not-so-ready to commit types. And now, just like that, she was supposed to forget everything for Christian — a man who lived miles away? They hadn't even grown close enough to consider it.

"Are you still there?" he asked.

"I am. Look, I think we should go take a long shower, settle in for the night, get some rest and wake up tomorrow with clear minds and a fresh perspective."

"You don't have to do that, Frankie."

"What? Long showers always help when I feel stressed," she said with a nervous chuckle.

"So now the topic of our relationship is stressful?" he said.

Frankie paused for a moment cautiously considering the right thing to say. She felt like she couldn't win, and questioned if she was going crazy or if he was just having a bad day.

Christian's tone shifted. "Nevermind, you're right, Frankie. I don't know why I thought we could have a conversation about our progression. I just wanted to see if we were on the same page, but clearly, you're not up for it. I'll take my cue and let it go. Let's just talk later in the week, after you get acclimatized to being back."

She carried the bucket over to the loveseat. "Christian, I didn't mean for you to —"

"It's fine, Frankie. Don't worry about it. Get some sleep."

To her surprise, Frankie stood listening to several clicks that eventually led to silence on the other end of the line — not exactly what she had in mind for an evening night cap with her boyfriend.

* * *

Taking a brisk walk on Friday mornings before work had become a thing for Frankie and Meg. In addition to the walks with her roommate, their favorite bookstore would be hosting another book club gathering in the evening. It may sound cheesy to some, but it was moments like these Frankie cherished most.

While squatting in the driveway to tighten her shoelaces, Frankie glanced up at Meg. "You don't know how much I've been looking forward to this. We have a lot of catching up to do, my friend."

"Tell me about it. I say we try and push for a couple of miles this morning. Maybe even make our way down to the shore and back? That way I can hear about your trip," Meg replied.

"Let's do it."

After a minute of settling into a rhythm, Meg nudged Frankie. "Sooo, spill it, already. How was Atlanta? Do you think Christian is on the verge of proposing?"

"Proposing? Oh, God no," Frankie snapped.

"Okayyy. Wow. Didn't think the idea of a proposal was such a terrible thing. Whatever happened to all the excitement you had when you were packing your bags?"

Frankie rolled her eyes. "You're starting to sound just as bad as Christian. I'm happy. I'm fine. I'm just — still trying to figure things out as we go. That's fair, don't you think?"

For some reason Frankie felt like she was trying to convince herself just as much as she was trying to convince Meg.

Meg smiled. "You can be honest with me. You're starting to lose that spark you once had, aren't you?"

Frankie slowed the pace, listening to the sound of gravel beneath her tennis shoes as they continued to walk. "Maybe I am. I don't know. I keep asking myself if I'm being realistic, dating someone who lives so far away. I mean, seriously Meg, at this rate I'm blowing through my sky miles and I don't feel any closer to Christian than when all of this began. And, to make matters worse, yesterday when I got back, he told me he loved me."

Frankie felt Meg's hand rest on her arm. "What did you say?" Meg asked.

"I froze and pretended like I didn't hear him. And, of course he picked up on it, addressing it later on the phone last night. I know it was the wrong move, but I didn't know what to say, Meg. I guess I just wanted to avoid hurting him."

"I know the feeling," Meg agreed.

Frankie's eyebrows raised. "Why? Is everything okay with you and Parker?"

"Yes, everything is fine. But, like yourself, I'm

wrestling with a few things. I know I should talk with him, but I can't seem to find the right words."

Frankie looked heavenward. "It almost seems silly — two grown women like ourselves struggling with talking to the men we care about. We really have to do better."

"Yes. And, speaking of doing better, why don't we start by identifying what Frankie wants for a change. Do you even know what you want in a relationship? Is this issue a you thing or is Christian the problem?"

Frankie drew in a deep breath. "It's not him. He's doing everything right. He's perfect in every way. I can't think of a single woman who wouldn't want a guy like Christian. It's me, not him."

When they arrived at the peak of the hill, Frankie could see the sidewalk that ran parallel to the light beige sand, spilling over into the blue water out in the distance. *Now this is paradise,* she thought.

"Focus," Meg snapped. "What do you mean when you say it's you and not him? You still want to find love someday, don't you?"

"Yes. But sometimes I question whether I'm fit for it. I feel like I'm damaged goods, too messed up in my head to handle being in a decent relationship no matter how hard I try."

Meg paused again. "Frankie, what would make you say such a thing?"

"Come on, keep walking," Frankie said, tugging at Meg's arm.

Admitting her shortcomings wasn't exactly an easy thing for Frankie to do. Especially when internally, she fought with an ongoing cycle of emotions, ranging from embarrassment, to self-inflicted fears.

Meg continued. "Frankie, it's so unlike you to talk like this. Since when did you become damaged goods?" Meg asked, using her fingers as air quotes.

Frankie's eyes widened. "My track record is filled with more failures than successes when it comes to relationships. It's to the point where I've come to expect the unhappy ending before it rears its ugly head. Take this situation for example. It's all my fault. I was cautious when I first met Christian and I should've stayed that way. But no, what did I do instead? I fell for the whole elevator rescue and the romantic gesture to travel back and forth to be together. Next thing I know, I'm dreaming of what life could be like with someone practically halfway across the globe. For what? I have no intentions of leaving the Bahamas. I'll never move to Atlanta to be with him."

Meg laughed. "Halfway across the globe? It's about a two-hour flight from here to Hartsfield Jackson International, what are you talking about?"

"You get the idea!" Frankie murmured.

"I get the idea, alright. You're just not that into him, which is fine. It's not the end of the world. But what I'm not going to tolerate is all this talk about you being damaged goods."

Silence fell between the two as Frankie flashed back to a time when life was a lot simpler. She envisioned a specific time when her parents were out of town and she stayed with a dear neighbor friend, Ms. Mable. She was more like a nanny than anything else. Since it was during the school year, Frankie lined up her school shoes in Ms. Mable's guest room from the most casual to the dressiest. Her favorite was a black patent leather pair which she always wore with white socks and lace trim. Lace always made her feel fancy. She always envisioned someday when she grew up, she would wear white lace to her wedding.

"Earth to Frankie," Meg teased.

"I hear you loud and clear. No more talk about being damaged goods. Got it. But something has to give, Meg. I can't seem to get it right. I'm like one of those hopeless romantics that falls in love with the idea of falling in love, but when it comes down to it—"

Meg squinted. "When it comes down to what?"

"When it comes down to it, I really don't know that I'm fit to be with anyone but myself," Frankie confessed. She continued looking straight ahead, noticing cars as they passed by. She knew her friend was probably dissecting every single word she'd spoken.

"Look, Meg. I'm a complex kind of girl. Always

have been and probably always will be. I'm not one of those people that get it right the first time and live life happily ever-after, till death do us part, or whatever else couples are vowing to each other nowadays. It's just the way things are for me. You on the other hand are living a fairytale dream. So please — uplift my spirits and fill me in on how things are going over at Seaside B&B."

Frankie felt Meg's eyes throw a sharp dagger.

"Nice way to transition off yourself and onto me, kiddo. You're not fooling anybody." Meg laughed.

"I know. You don't miss anything. But, for the love of all things good, tell me about the B&B anyway. I need a break from trying to figure out my love life with Christian — or lack thereof," Frankie explained, knowing she wouldn't dare broach the topic of the run-in she had with her old flame, David. What was the point? Yeah sure, he was staying at the same resort where she worked. She may have even looked up his room number out of curiosity. But, in the end she was certain the visit would be brief and they'd have no further interaction.

Besides, if Frankie dared open up, giving others a window into that aspect of her life, she'd only be revealing one more failed attempt at love. Not exactly something she was proud of.

Meg's mouth curved into a half smile. "Okay, I'll let you off the hook for now, but trust me when I tell you we're not done with this."

"Mm-hmm." Frankie nodded. "How's Parker doing and how's everything going at the B&B?"

"Parker's good. Despite the fact that we still have Mr. Barnes staying in one of the rooms and —"

"Still? I knew he was supposed to stay on site for a little while to help get the business on its feet, but wow. What about the guests? Have they noticed?" Frankie asked.

"No, not at all. He even has good days, every now and again, where he likes to come downstairs and sit at the front desk. And, trust me, Parker knows it's time to start talking about making other arrangements. But it's a delicate situation and I think he just wants to make sure he treads lightly."

"Yeah, that makes a lot of sense," Frankie said.

While picking up the tempo, Frankie probed Meg a little more. "And, how are you doing in your managerial role? Does it feel like everything is starting to fall into place?"

Meg frowned. "About that."

Frankie listened intently while trying to catch her breath. "Gee, I take one week off from speed walking and it feels like I'm out of shape."

Meg teased. "I hate to break it to you, but if you only walk once a week, you are definitely out of shape."

"Alright, wise guy. Continue on with your story," Frankie laughed.

"Frankie, I want to ask you a question. And, regardless of what the answer is, I need you to tell me the honest truth."

Feeling a small twitch in her stomach, Frankie responded. "Sure, what's up?"

"Do you think I did the right thing by going to work at the B&B?" Meg asked.

"What do you mean? Of course I think you did the right thing. You were able to free yourself to go carry out your dreams of being an owner someday."

"I — I know, but."

Frankie's eyes narrowed. "But what? Are you two going through a rough patch?"

She asked, stopping alongside Meg.

"No. Not really."

Frankie's eyes widened. "Okay, well I'm at a loss here. What would make you question your decision to work at the B&B? Alongside the man you love, no less. I don't get it."

With her hands clasped behind her head, Meg confessed "At first glance, yeah sure, everything is perfect. No reason to complain. But I feel like prior to joining worlds with Parker there was a clear separation between our work life and our relationship. Now, not-so-much. In order to help pick up the slack at the B&B, I've been his housekeeper, his bookkeeper, his manager, and even his errand girl. And, in return, it's like the relationship is taking a back seat to the business. Correction, there are the occasional signs of affection in passing, maybe even an occasional pat on the rump, but things have definitely changed."

Frankie chuckled. "Sorry. The whole pat on the rump part... it's such a guy thing," she said, then quickly changed her tune. "Meg, is there really an issue? Or is this just you having to adjust to working with your —"

"With my what?" Meg interrupted. "My boyfriend, who I rarely get to date anymore? Yeah, I guess you're right, I'm struggling big time with this. I can't help but wonder if I'm getting in too deep on the business side of things without being committed to him first, or at least better defining some boundaries," she said, now clasping her hands over her head. "Should I be investing so much time and energy into a man who's married to his business more than he is to me?"

Frankie's hands slipped to her waist. "Whoa. You need to take a deep breath and think this through. I don't really think Parker is more committed to his business than he is to you. He's probably just caught up in wanting to make sure things run smoothly. After all, this was a huge undertaking."

Meg nodded. "You're right. I'm probably being irrational, maybe even overthinking things. Maybe I should just play it by ear and see how the dust settles between us, right?"

Frankie signaled Meg to pick up the pace. "Wrong. Not that I'm in the position to give advice, but my motto is balance in all things. Talk to the man. This way you can be certain you're on the same page about your future. Don't go overboard, assuming the worst before he's had a chance to weigh in with his input. Make sense?"

Meg slid her arm around her friend's shoulder, giving her a big side squeeze. "Makes a lot of sense. I don't know why I'm so quick to drum up these crazy ideas in my head. I'm grateful for you. Blame it on my hormones. Lately they've been all out of whack. Thank you for keeping me grounded, my friend," Meg smiled.

"Good. I'm glad to be of service. Now, if we're ever going to finish this walk before my ten o'clock teleconference then we really need to step things up," Frankie said, but as she spoke, she noticed her friend's attention shifting across the street. "Meg?"

The distorted look on Meg's face as she stared led Frankie to trace her glare. "What are you looking at?" she asked.

When Frankie turned around, the view of Parker escorting a beautiful woman down the street was enough to make them both pause, leaving them both speechless.

Chapter 4

Frankie

"I pulled up the file for you," Frankie's assistant, Bree, sang in a melodious tone.

"Thanks, Bree," Frankie responded. "I'm pulling into the parking lot as we speak. I always think it's amazing how everyone else gets to enjoy their telework days without interruption, but the moment I'm scheduled to work from home, chaos breaks loose."

"I'm sorry, Frankie. What's a girl to do? If the CEO calls and says he wants to drop by, my guess is everyone would want to be here. No?"

Frankie placed one hand over her chest. "You're right, Bree. Listen, if I don't say it enough, I'm forever grateful for the way you always look out for me. Ever since I was promoted to director, you've literally had my back every step of the way. I don't know what I'd do without you."

"That's what I'm here for, Boss. Just don't forget about me around bonus season." She giggled.

"I hear you loud and clear, Bree. We'll talk about your bonus, but for now I'm pulling into my space. I'll be upstairs in five minutes."

"See you, then."

As the line disconnected, Frankie tucked away her sunglasses and pulled into her reserved spot. The new role had come with its perks including a parking space, a new office on the oceanside of the resort, and telework days which she normally used at her discretion.

Outside of the new title, and boatload of additional responsibilities, she loved being the director of HR at a five-star resort. For Frankie, coming from such humble beginnings, it was a significant sign of growth.

While waiting for the elevator, thoughts of Christian ran through her mind. Eventually one of them would have to break the awkwardness between them by picking up the phone and calling. Someone would have to be the bigger person. She just wasn't sure who it would be.

Inside the elevator, Frankie mashed the button for the fifth floor, but stood back as a hand stopped the doors from closing. She looked up. "Grant, perfect timing," she said to her boss while noticing David following behind him.

Oh, my God.

Frankie's heartbeat thrusted in her chest at a crazy rhythm, causing her to feel rattled.

Her boss smiled. "There you are. We were just heading up to the fifth floor to come see you."

"We?" Frankie asked.

"Yes. Forgive me. This is my friend and labor attorney, David Sullivan. He's staying here at the resort this week. I thought it might be nice to solicit some of his expert advice."

"Advice?" Frankie questioned, in a deflated voice. Her eyes locked with David's as her boss chimed in. "Yes, I figured since David is a labor attorney, licensed to practice here in Nassau, I should get his advice and —" He paused. "I'm sorry. I should probably start by introducing you two, even though the way you're looking at each other it seems you've already met."

With a raised brow, Frankie patiently waited for David to explain.

Still gazing into her eyes, he belted out a startling chuckle. "Frankie, what a surprise."

The nerve, she thought.

"Hello, David. Long time no see."

Seemingly intrigued, Grant continued to gaze. "How do you two know each other?"

Frankie proceeded to explain but was interrupted by David. "We're old friends."

"Yep, old friends," she added. "Back from my days of living in New York. It's been a long time. Right David?"

"Yes. A very long time," he noted as the door opened on the fifth floor. As they stepped into the hall he continued. "After all these years who would've thought our paths would cross here, of all places."

Frankie hoped with every ounce of her being he'd read between the lines, staying far away from mentioning any intimate details. So far, she liked the way he was playing along.

Grant continued, "Well, this is even better than expected. Since we're all familiar we can cut right to the chase. Frankie is the director of Human Resources. A darn good director if I might add. Everything concerning labor laws comes through her office first before it hits my desk. We have an outstanding case that I'd love for you to review if you have the time, David. I'd like to compare notes and get your thoughts about what our current lawyer is advising us to do." Grant then shifted toward Frankie. "You know the case I'm referring to, right?"

She perked up. "Yes. Bree pulled the file for me this morning. I'm certain it's waiting on my desk."

"Perfect. If you wouldn't mind taking David with you to look things over, I would greatly appreciate it.

I need to make a pit stop at our CFO's office and then I'll be right in."

This day keeps getting better and better, she thought.

"Frankie, is that okay with you?" her boss asked, catching her in the middle of a bewildered stare.

"Yes, of course. We'll be in my office."

She then adjusted the shoulder straps of her bag and addressed David. "Right this way."

If there were ever a moment where Frankie felt God had a sense of humor, the time had certainly come. Her past mistakes always had a way of rearing its ugly head, reminding her of all that had gone wrong.

"Hi Bree, if you don't mind, please hold all of my calls. I'll be meeting with Mr. Sullivan, one of Grant's advisors. Grant is down the hall and should be joining us in a few minutes."

Bree nodded. "Hold all calls, I'm on it. Mr. Sullivan, can I offer you a bottle of water?"

He waved. "I'm good. Thank you."

Once behind closed doors Frankie took a brief glance at the calming view of the Palm trees swaying outside before turning around. "Please, have a seat. Make yourself comfortable."

David locked eyes with her. "Frankie, before we get started, I just want to say I had no idea."

"Are you sure about that? Because that's not what

it looks like to me. First you follow me on the shuttle, now this," she snarled.

He reared his head back a bit. "So, you think I'm stalking you? Why on earth would I do that? I haven't seen you in God knows how long. That's not my style and you know it."

Frankie's eyes burned with passion. "Well, then by all means, please enlighten me. How did you manage to find your way to the same island, at the same exact resort as me, and wait for it — in my office!"

"Grant told you how. We're old work buddies. He knew I was staying at the resort this week and he asked me for a little friendly advice. Afterwards we're going to grab a bite and that's it. The rest is history," he explained.

"If that's all there is to it, what's this about you being licensed to practice here in Nassau?"

She watched as his face turned flush, looking as if he were caught in the middle of a lie.

But, instead of explaining himself he sat down, and slouched back in her chair. "Isn't there a file you wanted me to review?"

She felt the impulse to tell him a thing or two rising in her flesh. But she didn't. Instead, she folded her arms and simply waited.

"What?" he said. "Why should I have to explain myself? It's not like you care anyway. As I said earlier, the only reason I'm here is because Grant asked me to be. And, if you don't want to look foolish in front of your boss when he walks in, I suggest we start discussing the contents of this case."

Her eyebrows folded. "You are so —"

Before she could complete her thought, Grant passed by her glass window and popped his head in. "Guys, I hate to have to do this, but I need to reschedule this meeting for another day this week. My wife just called in a state of hysteria."

Frankie tilted her head. "Is everything okay?"

"Yes, it's a good kind of hysteria. Apparently, our granddaughter is arriving earlier than expected. They're at the hospital now and I'm under strict orders to get over there before I miss the whole thing."

Frankie smiled as she watched David extend a handshake. "Aww, how exciting. Please express my thoughts of love to the family, and when you get a chance, send pictures."

"Will do. Hey, since David is already here, there's no point in wasting his time. Why don't the two of you look things over for me and give me your feedback this week."

Frankie glanced at her unwanted guest. "Uhh."

"As a matter of fact, go ahead and grab lunch downstairs while you're at it. Frankie, tell the manager the tab is on me. I feel terrible about skipping out on this meeting. This is the least I can do," Grant said.

The least you can do? What do you mean the least you can do?

David stood up. "Grant, that's not necessary. You and I can always catch up sometime soon. We can even grab cigars in celebration of your new grandbaby."

Frankie watched as Grant slapped his hand down on David's shoulder. She knew her boss well enough to know he was definitely going to have the final word. "Agreed. But still, it would mean the world to me if you would mull over the case over a nice meal here at The Cove. I won't take no for an answer."

Forcing her best smile she said, "Not to worry, Grant. We'll take care of everything here. Go and be with your family and give everyone our regards."

* * *

With occasional nods and grunting noises, David combed through the paperwork, grabbed a pen, and made notes. Frankie, on the other hand, was still stewing over their unresolved conversation and pending appointment to eat together.

He glanced her way. "We can skip out on lunch. It's not a big deal."

"Hmm. While the idea sounds appealing, Grant would never let me hear the end of it," she snarled.

He slid the file onto her desk. "You know, I can't

seem to figure out why you have so much pent-up animosity towards me. Again, you're the one who broke things off and left, not me."

She motioned her hands as if playing an imaginary violin. "You've reminded me of this already. Last time I checked there was a justified reason for it. And, that has nothing to do with why you're here, in my office, today."

She watched as David shifted, returning to a relaxed position. "A justified reason? Oh, I'd really like to hear this one. Please, enlighten me," he said.

With a failed attempt at initiating her mental countdown, Frankie could feel her temperature rising. "This is insane."

"What's so insane about it? We were engaged, Frankie. Normally, people don't just walk away from something that serious without trying to work through it."

She eased to the edge of her chair, throwing him a dagger that was sharper than a two-edged sword. "I'm not sure why you insist on rehashing this. Some things are meant to remain in the past for good."

With a look of frustration, he stood up. "Fine, have it your way." Acknowledging the file, he said, "Tell Grant I think his attorney is steering him in the right direction. While there are a couple of things I might do differently, overall, I think he has a strong case. As for you, I'd sit down with the legal team, answer whatever questions they have and let them guide you from there."

Feeling surprised at the swift shift, she responded, "Okay."

He continued, "And, to answer your question about why I'm here, Grant is letting me stay at the resort this week while I search for a place to live. I'm planting roots here on the island. But, don't worry, I'll be sure to stay out of your way."

Frankie couldn't understand why it felt like she'd been sucker punched in the gut. Was David a bad man? No. In fact they'd lived out their time in New York together on a natural high, feeling unstoppable. Their romance was a whirlwind, to sort of speak. They were introduced through a friend of her cousin, they became fast friends, then one day that friendship turned into serious lovers.

Looking toward the plaque with her title on the desk, guilt washed over Frankie. "David."

"Not to worry. I'm leaving now," he said, surrendering his hands.

"No. That's not what I was going to say," she offered. "Actually — I owe you an apology. When Grant escorted you to the fifth floor, and explained that you were here on business, I should've been professional — even behind closed doors. It's my job to represent company business before personal business. I'm sorry."

He cracked a smile. "It's all good. I'm almost certain I hit a nerve at the airport. So, I can't say that I blame you."

"You definitely hit a nerve, but thank you for being understanding."

They stood awkwardly for another minute before he started heading for the door. "I'll see you around, Frankie."

While it would've been easy to let him go, she thought better of it, deciding to carry out Grant's request.

Moving quickly to the other side of the desk she reached out. "Hey, wait a minute. Grant left specific orders about lunch, remember?"

As David turned around, she found herself within close proximity of his body, his masculine scent, and the warmth of his breath. It was electrifying and everything she needed to bring back fresh memories of their yearlong romance — fresh memories of their almost forever love.

David looked deeply into her eyes, which made her stare just as intently into his.

Frankie, don't do it. Don't you dare do it, she thought.

He inched closer, seemingly preparing to seize the vulnerable moment when someone knocked on the door and busted in.

"So sorry to interrupt, Boss," Bree said, catching their intimate moment. "I'm sorry. I can come back."

Frankie motioned. "No, Bree. It's fine. What's the matter?"

She hesitated, glancing back and forth between them. "I know you asked me to hold your calls, but Grant wanted me to relay the message. His granddaughter just arrived. He didn't quite make it to the hospital yet, but her name is Charlotte and she's seven pounds, eight ounces." She giggled.

Quickly shuffling to create a safe distance, Frankie's eyes lit up. "That's wonderful news. I'm sure he's feeling like such a proud grandpa. If you wouldn't mind, can you send an arrangement to the house on behalf of the department, Bree?"

"I'm on it." Bree smirked looking at David. "While I'm working on that, hopefully you two are heading downstairs to beat the midday rush."

Frankie intervened. "The midday rush?"

"Yes, Grant asked me to catch you guys before you left for lunch."

"Ahh, yes. We were just heading that way now, weren't we David?"

David glanced at his watch. "Actually, if it's okay with you I'm going to take a raincheck. There's something important that I really should take care of. If Grant asks, tell him it was my fault."

Feeling confused, Frankie responded, "Sure. No need to explain. I'm sure you guys can reschedule something soon."

After his polite departure, Frankie stood bewildered, wondering what an almost kiss would've felt like coming from the man she almost married.***

"Boss, I'm not one to pry but —"

"Bree, who are we kidding here?" Frankie teased, laughing it off.

Frankie returned to the window behind her desk, overlooking the grounds of the resort. If only Bree's footsteps weren't coming closer Frankie might be able to sit and quietly think things through. Why had she almost fallen into the lips of another man? How is it that David went from plucking her last nerve to sending electrifying shockwaves through a brief, yet close encounter?

On the other hand, who could blame Bree for wanting to stick around? Who wouldn't want an explanation as to why their boss was on the verge of locking lips with the CEO's friend?

"Is everything okay, Boss?"

"Everything's fine, Bree. Why do you ask?" Frankie said, turning around.

Bree gave her a blank stare. The kind of stare that said 'you're not fooling anybody, so you might as well come clean'.

"Was it that obvious?" Frankie winced.

"Obvious is an understatement." With arms crossed over her chest, Bree continued. "So, how do you know the hot lawyer? And, why on earth did you let him get away without having lunch?"

"You swear you won't tell?" Frankie blushed.

Frankie and Bree always shared a healthy balance between being professionals and work besties. It was a relationship that was rare among those who were always working against each other, trying to claw their way to the top.

"I swear I won't say one word."

Standing with hands clasped behind her back, Frankie explained. "We used to be an item a long time ago, but things didn't work out between us. And, as my luck would have it, apparently he knows Grant... and as you know, Grant wants advice from David about this case. That's pretty much everything in a nutshell."

Bree lifted a finger. "Oh, no. There has to be more to it than that. When I walked in you were practically swapping saliva with each other. This is way more than just a coincidental reunion."

Frankie's cheeks turned three shades of red. "Bree, now you're exaggerating. Were we standing close? Yes. But that's all there was to it," she said, lying to herself.

"Okay, Boss, you keep telling yourself that." Bree laughed. "Oh, and before I forget. While you were in your meeting, Christian called."

Slouching into her chair, Frankie replied, "Oh."

"Interesting response."

"Oh, Bree."

"Seriously. A minute ago when you were talking about David, although in denial, your eyes lit up like the Fourth of July. The moment I mention Christian, the only thing you can come up with is 'oh.' What's that all about?"

Frankie placed her hands firmly on the desk and leaned in. "Bree, surely we have some new hires that need to be processed, or benefits that need looking over."

Bree raised up, and pushed in her chair. "Okay, Boss. I can take a hint. Just know you're not fooling anybody. I plan on getting it out of you at some point."

Frankie watched as Bree slipped out of her office with a silly smirk smeared across her face. She knew she wouldn't repeat anything to the staff, but that was the least of her concern. As she sank into her plush leather chair, the thing that replayed constantly in her mental space was the events leading to the breakup. Over and over again, she heard herself rehearsing her breakup speech. Back then, Frankie confidently told herself she was doing the right thing. So, why was it claiming so much real estate in her mind now?

* * *

"May I have a glass of cranberry juice with my meal?" Frankie asked.

"Sure, Hun. One cranberry juice coming right up," her server replied

With a long Friday in the rearview mirror and a last-minute cancellation to go to the book club with Meg, the least Frankie could do was treat herself to a solo meal down at the Tiki Bar.

If she wasn't an employee for the resort, it would almost feel ridiculous, sitting there all alone. But, like most, she was entertained by her cell phone while she waited, and even more entertained at the idea of not having to cook.

Scrolling through she noticed a missed text message from Christian that read, "Flying out on a last minute trip out of the country. Chasing a big story that could be a game changer for a possible promotion. Will try and reach out once I get settled."

Interesting, she thought.

"Is this seat taken?" a deep voice asked, startling the daylights out of her.

Frankie gripped her phone, allowing a serious face to give way to a subtle smile. "I guess it is now."

Again, she caught a fresh whiff of whatever cologne David was wearing. This time she resisted the temptation to inhale. "So, you decided to come grab a bite after all. Earlier you seemed like you were in quite the rush."

Exposing a dimple he replied, "Not quite. I was

heading out for an evening walk when I saw you sitting here. So, I decided to stop by and take a chance on saying hello. As for earlier, I knew you really didn't want to have lunch with me. I figured I'd make things easy on you."

Frankie's mouth fell open. "Make things easier on me or make things easier on yourself?"

"No, I meant what I said the first time. I can tell when a woman is not interested in dining with me. Even if she happens to be the former love of my life."

"So, you're not going to let that whole thing go, are you?"

He laughed. "It's the truth. I see no point in denying it."

When the server returned, she delivered Frankie's cranberry juice and chicken basket with fries.

"Thank you." Frankie glanced upward. "If you don't mind, can I have a to-go box for the food?"

"Sure. One to-go box coming right up."

A brief glance at David revealed that he was watching her every move. "What?"

He smiled, looking down. "Nothing, it's just good to see you again, that's all. Your smile, your mannerisms — it's nice to see that none of those things have really changed."

"David," Frankie said in a low voice.

"I know. I don't want to overstep my boundaries."

He stood back up. "I was just stopping by for a brief hello, that's all."

She looked up at his rugged beard and allowed her eyes to trace his physique for one long minute before gently tapping his chair. "Have a seat. I agree. It's been a long time. The least we can do is chat over a drink."

Chapter 5

Meg

Meg sat at the front desk, catching a glimpse of the sunset as she mulled over several resumes. At least that's what she was trying to do. She'd spent most of the day quietly spewing over Parker's outing with Portia Fennley. It wasn't the fact that he'd taken her somewhere, but more so, he hadn't mentioned a thing about it.

Since when do guests get personally escorted around the island? she thought.

It's not like the woman had a low profile. She was blond, gorgeous, wore excessive jewels, making it easy for Meg or anyone else to see them together.

In her mind, there had to be some sort of explanation as to why Parker would personally escort her anywhere. Especially if it meant leaving the B&B under the supervision of Mr. Barnes.

The mere fact that Barnes was out of his room was a miracle, and usually a sign that he was in good spirits. On good days, he came out of his room, looking for opportunities to fill in, just like he used to when he was the owner. On bad days, he stayed in his room, which happened more often than not.

The only problem with all this is Parker had been too preoccupied, not realizing just how annoyed Meg was becoming.

As she watched the sunset, he appeared. "There you are. I was starting to wonder if I was going to see you at all today," she said, watching Parker as he approached carrying the picture frame from the basement."

"It's definitely been busy today, and that's probably an understatement." He then glanced at the clock. "It's way past the time you normally head out of here. Thank you for putting in the extra hours today. The additional help certainly hasn't gone unnoticed," he said. Parker then leaned over, pausing to kiss her on the forehead.

"No problem." Meg's brows furrowed.

Parker fixed his attention on the resumes. "Anything promising in the pile? I'd hate to see another month go by without getting some help with housekeeping. Miguel and my sister, Savannah, are ready to get things rocking and rolling with the redesign of the second property. I just need this house to be fully staffed first."

According to Parker, the business plan had been meticulously revised and was ready for execution. He allowed room in the budget for minor, yet refreshing updates to the main house of Seaside B&B. As for the rest of the property, fresh paint would bring the gift shop to life, and the most in depth demolition would take place on house number two. In his mind, it was the perfect balance to keep the income flowing while giving the B&B the makeover it needed.

Meg tried hard to suppress her fingernail tapping on the wooden desk. "If I come across something good, I'll let you know."

On the inside, her heart was secretly aching inside her chest. It was the way she always felt when imagining the worst.

As Parker started to pick up the frame again, he said, "Hey, I'm going to dust this thing off and get it ready to show Barnes tomorrow. If you wouldn't mind locking up on your way out, I'd appreciate it."

"Okay, but before you go — I was wondering if you had a minute to talk?" she asked.

With a half-energized smile, he replied, "What's up?"

"This morning I was taking a walk with Frankie. We were walking along the beach. You know, the stretch not far from her house."

"Mm-hmm."

Suddenly feeling stupid, Meg paused to think about it. The last thing she needed was to miscalculate her words, making it seem like she was accusing him of something.

Parker chimed in. "Everything okay?"

"Um, yeah. It's just — I could've sworn I saw you on the other side of the road, going into one of the shops with Mrs. Fennley. Thought you might have mentioned something about it by now," she said, giving off a nervous chuckle.

Waving it off, he kept moving toward the door. "Yeah, about that. She came down here all flustered this morning, mentioning something about being out of emergency toiletries. Next thing I know, that turned into wanting to stop by one store after the other. I don't think the woman takes too kindly to the word no."

"Can't Mr. Fennley help take care of that?" Meg asked.

"It feels like I haven't seen the guy come out of his room since they arrived. I didn't want to pry, but from everything she mentioned, I think they're still at odds. All I know is she came flailing out here as if her world was coming to an end, and since Barnes was already by the front desk —"

Meg sighed. "You came running to her aid."

"What was I supposed to do, Meg?"

Mentally, she calculated a list of ideas. *Call a cab, hitch hike, walk. You name it, just stay out of my man's way,* she thought.

"Well, that was nice of you, but it wouldn't hurt

for her to learn her way around the island like the other guests do. I'm sure a local car service would be glad to pick her up if she doesn't want to explore on foot."

Why she would ever allow that statement to roll off her tongue was more than Meg could figure out. She hadn't intended to display any form of jealousy. Her real feelings were rooted in a much deeper issue. A heart-to-heart issue that she and Parker would need to address real soon.

"Good evening, Meg," Portia Fennley, belted out, startling Meg in the middle of their conversation.

Meg turned three shades of red, wondering why Parker hadn't given her a warning. "Why hello, Mrs. Fennley. How's everything in your room this evening?" she asked.

Mrs. Fennley glanced over at Parker, then turned back. "The room is fine, but I was wondering if you had a fresh assortment of tea bags. Tea always seems to soothe me right before I go to bed."

Verbally Meg heard the word tea, but from the look of her evening attire the woman wanted to be soothed by so much more. A double take was all Meg needed to notice her satin pajama set, fuzzy slippers, and the look in Parker's eyes as he noticed.

He immediately spoke up. "No problem, I'm happy to —"

But Meg slipped from around the desk, signaling to Parker that she had it under control. "I'll bring an assortment of tea bags to your room. How about I meet you upstairs in let's say, five minutes?" She smiled.

Now, Meg realized she could've been reaching out on a limb here. But she didn't think her suspicions were far off. This woman was fishing around for something besides tea, and Parker Wilson wasn't about to become her next catch.

* * *

Once Meg returned from delivering Mrs. Fennley's tea, she locked eyes with Parker. "We need to talk."

Meg's temples throbbed at the onset of a headache ratcheting up, but she ignored it. There were too many things between them that needed to be clearly defined.

"Meg, I already told you the outing earlier today was no big deal."

"It's about us, Parker."

"Okay. What about us?"

A wave of nausea washed over her stomach. It was likely because she hadn't eaten in hours plus a terrible little concert was drumming up in her head. But she pressed on just the same. "I need to know that we're okay, that we're solid in our relationship and that we won't let this business come between us."

"Whoa. Where's all this coming from? The way I see it, everything is just fine," he replied.

She scowled. "Fine? I don't think so. Sure, we get along great, and there's nothing like being able to see each other whenever we want, but every waking hour of the day, we're working. When was the last time we carved out dedicated time for ourselves?"

He paced to the other side of the foyer. "I don't know what to say. You knew when you joined me in this venture it was going to take a lot of dedicated time to help this business get on its feet. I'm not saying that we're not important, but there's a lot at stake here. You do understand that, don't you?"

She agreed there was a lot at stake, but he truly didn't know the half. While she was busy fulfilling various roles such as manager, housekeeper, bookkeeper, and on occasion part time cook, she was silently going through some things. Things she hadn't even shared with Frankie. Her hormones were shifting, her body was changing, and her most recent pregnancy test revealed that she was with child. Well, the result wasn't exactly crystal clear. But it wasn't a clear no either.

"I understand that. However, it's still no excuse. We still need to be intentional about carving out time to maintain what we have together."

He looked at her as if she were delusional.

"Okay, Parker. I'm just going to lay everything on the line. We're part-time lovers and more than full-time business owners. Something has to give. Yes, we're occasionally affectionate, but then it's right back to another task."

She calculated her next set of thoughts meticulously, knowing that once she said it, there was no taking it back.

"It just feels like you're growing more committed to the B&B and not to me. And, speaking of commitment to one another, I'm starting to feel like the help instead of the woman you fell in love with."

The words were finally out for Parker's full consumption, digestion, and reaction. May admittedly had been the worst time of day, given they were both tired, but when else would she have a chance to speak to him?

"Wow. The help. I see. Well, if anything, I'm grateful for your honesty. It looks like I have some soul searching to do. So far it looks as if my best just hasn't been good enough."

"Parker, come on. Don't make it sound like that."

She practically wanted to kick herself for not addressing the most pressing issue of all. But, technically she was still doubtful about bringing it up. After all, the pregnancy test was one of the cheap brands from the convenience store. And, when one has to question whether the negative lines are positive, or the positive lines are negative, it's definitely a sign to purchase a higher quality test.

She continued. "When I agreed to come here and work with you, I never considered the impact it would have on us. I need reassurance that we're going to put ourselves first, no matter how busy it gets here at the B&B. Think about it. We did it before, so why would anything change now?"

He came closer, sliding his hand down the side of her arm. "You're right. We can do better... Specifically, I can do better," he said, cupping her face between his hands. "I'm operating on new territory here, trying my best to keep us afloat while learning the ropes."

Meg's eyes scanned down to his collar and back up to his eyes again. "And, you're doing an amazing job. You really are. It's just, in the midst of everything we have going on, I think I'm —" She hesitated.

"What? Don't hold back. Talk to me."

"Parker, I think I'm —"

Unfortunately, the sound of a hard thump from the floor above put an abrupt end to their conversation.

Chapter 6

Frankie

Frankie found herself lost in the ebb and flow of David's lips dancing with hers. He had a way of drawing her in, then letting go, then teasing her all over again with another soft, succulent kiss.

How in the world? she thought.

How in the world did one go from sitting at the bar over a light meal, catching up over old times, and taking a walk under the moonlight, to this. How would she explain this to Christian? On second thought, she couldn't worry about Christian at the moment. Instead, how would she justify this with herself?

Frankie gently pulled away. "David, what are we doing?"

"My guess is we're finishing what we started a

long time ago. Or at least curious about it. I know I'm not the only one who felt something earlier today. It's one of the other reasons why I had to leave."

"Ah, and the entire truth comes out," she said, relaxing a little.

He chuckled, revealing that handsome smile she'd always adored. "No, I had a few things to do. I just shifted my schedule around, that's all."

"Mm-hmm. Sure. Blame it on your schedule, on me not wanting to have lunch, and a bunch of other excuses while you're at it."

His eyes turned somber. "Frankie."

"Yes?" she whispered.

"I... never... stopped... loving you. Never. I know you're not going to want to hear this, but you had it all wrong the day you left me."

She looked off into the distance. "Oh, here we go again. Look, I'm sorry, but this was a mistake. I allowed myself to get too comfortable while reminiscing over soft drinks. But I won't let it happen again."

David slipped his hands in his pockets. "Why do you always have guard rails up, Frankie?"

"Guard rails?"

After a long sigh, he said, "Yes, you always have your guard up. Except what you fail to realize is the last time you were so guarded, it actually cost you everything."

"Everything?" she exclaimed.

"Yes, it cost you a lifetime of love and happiness. But for some reason you're the only one who can't seem to see that." He nodded.

She reared her head back. "A little presumptuous, don't you think?"

"No. Nowhere close to being presumptuous, and here's why — Where is he now? Where's your knight and shining armor? The one you left me for."

The way he looked around as if searching for someone was enough to make her blood boil. But instead she counted.

He raised his hand to his ear. "What was that? I can't hear you."

"You know what, David. You are the most pompous, arrogant, son of a —"

"Whoa. Hold on now. Don't get mad at me for telling the truth."

It was all coming back to her now. The attorney side of his personality could argue until the cows came home. And, he did it so naturally. Although, in most cases he was usually correct and she was the one simply being stubborn.

Those type of arguments were the best back then, always leading to a really good make-up.

She noticed him glancing at her ring finger. "Don't go there, David. A ring doesn't define me as a woman. It never has and it never will."

His voice softened. "I never said it had to define

you, but I'm right when I say you never found the right one."

"What's your point?" she snapped.

If Frankie wasn't good at anything else, she definitely knew all the trigger words to push him over the edge. It wouldn't take long before she'd have him wishing he never stopped by to say hello.

"You broke off our engagement because I asked for a little more time, Frankie. A little more time was all I needed. A year or maybe a year and a half at best. I was struggling back then, Frankie. Drowning in a sea of student loans, in need of a better paying job, and newly engaged to a wonderful woman in the most expensive city in New York. You meant everything to me, but what did I get in return? Someone who didn't believe me and took off at the first sign of a setback."

With her stomach twisted in knots she argued. "That's not fair. You can't blame all this on me. How quickly you forget. In the end you were gone, practically twenty-four-seven supposedly working all hours of the night."

"Yes, trying to climb my way up so I could pay down the bills and save to start a new life with you. You know what, Frankie. I'll give you this much. I could've done things different. I could've held off the proposal until after everything was all squared away. But I wanted to show you how serious I was. I wanted to show you I was a man of my word. The only problem is I had no idea you would just leave me high and dry."

Frankie could deny what he was saying all night long if she wanted, but the man was reading her like a book. If she were being honest with herself, she had run from each and every guy she'd ever grown close to. Some received pink slips due to dishonesty or unfaithfulness. But for others, there was no explanation other than she was simply guarded, like David said. Growing up as a little girl in the UK, and watching her parents go through a divorce, was enough to keep her parked in neutral. Potentially forever.

The only problem was, in this instance, David was someone she truly loved.

She snarled back. "So, what? You never moved on to find the woman of your dreams? Someone who wouldn't leave you high and dry."

David looked her square in the eyes. "I got engaged again, but we eventually called it off. It was a mutual decision made by two people who just didn't belong together."

"Mmm."

"What about yourself?" he asked.

Holding up her ring finger as he so eloquently pointed out. "Flying solo, just like you said. Well, I should take that back. I actually have a boyfriend or — had a boyfriend, who lives in Atlanta. However, I'm almost certain after a recent turn of events he won't want much to do with me."

David chuckled, then quickly pretended to clear his throat. "Atlanta? That's quite a distance from here."

"Tell me about it."

"Plus, he probably wouldn't be too thrilled about you kissing me."

Frankie removed her purse from her shoulder, playfully swatting him with it. There was a love language that existed between them that was unspoken. A language that only they understood. The part Frankie found to be most intriguing was the electricity they still shared. There was no doubt it still existed, penetrating the very core of her being.

* * *

Laying in the sand under the moonlight felt dreamy. Making sand angels and resting on beach towels beside David wasn't exactly how Frankie envisioned her evening going, but her curiosity led her this far, so why not explore?

"I guess I owe you an apology," she said. "Back then I was young, immature, and most of all afraid. Never really having an example of what a good marriage looked like. I misjudged you, then called myself bailing before you did."

Counting the stars as she spoke was the only way Frankie could get through such a nerve-wracking confession. Everything she admitted was true.

Whether he'd understand or not was up for his interpretation.

"What made you think I would ever bail on you? Prior to proposing I was already committed. I was in it for the long haul."

Frankie tilted her head toward him. "The way you explain it today makes everything sound so easy. But, it didn't feel that way back then, David. It felt like you put the ring on my finger for security, then got lost in the world of your work life. In the interim, I didn't know what was going on. One moment I was living a fantasy. The next, it felt like you were whisked away, leaving me to figure out life in New York by myself."

He locked eyes with her. "That's not fair. I didn't leave you by yourself. You had your cousin as well, and I always made it known that my crazy work life would only be temporary. I just needed a little more time."

Rehashing the raw memories of their breakup nearly brought tears to her eyes. Was she supposed to feel this way? Was she supposed to care about a love she once had years ago?

She changed the subject. "So, you never told me. How did you manage to end up all the way out here on the island?"

"I started vacationing here about six years ago. But, about three years later I got a call from my boss asking me to help out one of his friends and give input on an employee litigation case. One thing led to another with that case, and a few others. Next thing you know I passed the bar and made the decision to move." He chuckled. "I never thought I'd live on an island until I was ready to retire. It's funny how quickly life can change."

With hands clasped behind her head she gave a nod. "Yeah, I'll bet. So, how did you end up meeting Grant?"

"Grant is friends with the CEO I was originally working with while on vacation. One day we started shooting the breeze and we just hit it off. To this day, I think he'd hire me for my services in a heartbeat if I ever offered. But I just can't bring myself to do it. I'm looking forward to working remotely and slowing down the pace from city living."

The sound of the night security's golf cart cruised by but didn't linger long. Frankie was all too familiar with the routine. He'd drive by, perusing the premises, barely noticing them if they lied still.

In disbelief she continued. "To this day, I still don't know how it happened, David."

"How what happened?"

She could feel his eyes piercing through her peripheral vision. "I don't know how I fell so madly in love with you back then. Within six months I would've given up everything to be your wife and to have your child. I loved hard back then. Yet, in the end I left, feeling like such a fool."

"What's wrong with loving someone? Especially if they love you even more in return? I don't get it. You're the only woman I know who talks about falling in love like it's an unattainable dream."

Visions of the day her mother sat her down to explain their final divorce rang through her mind like a bad, bad symphony.

"I guess there are some things we'll never understand," she said.

David rolled to his side, now staring directly at her. "Sorry, but I'm not buying it. To me, that sounds like a complete cop out."

"Okay, Mr. Know it all. What would you suggest that I have done differently?" she asked in a snarky tone.

"You ever heard of taking a leap of faith? What you need in your life is a real man to show you what real love looks like."

Hoisting herself up on her elbows she responded. "You sound so confident. So sure that what you're preaching makes perfect sense," she said.

"That's because I am confident. I'm a hopeless romantic at heart. Always have been and always will be."

Shifting her gaze directly at him. "If that's the case, why are you lying here, still single, just like me?"

He laughed loud enough to echo. "Frankie, you don't have to answer this now. But, I want you to think about it long and hard. Do you really believe it's a coincidence that we'd end up on the same island together? Of all the places to live and all these years later?"

Her eyebrows folded like a tightly knit accordion as she considered his words. What a puzzling question to ask. But, not more puzzling than watching his laughter dissipate and shift to the most intimate kiss she'd experienced in a very long time.

Chapter 7

Parker

Parker lost his train of thought as he listened to the doctor call Mr. Barnes' time of death. After transporting him by ambulance and placing him under breathing contraptions, and cords, there was nothing more they could do.

He stared at his lifeless hand draped over the side of the hospital bed, hoping for the slightest movement to indicate they were wrong. Regrettably, they weren't.

The nurse muttered something, then the doctor offered his condolences, but all Parker could do was envision the day he met Mr. Barnes, and how he was now laying there lifeless.

As the nurse continued to stare, Parker finally aligned his eyes with hers. "Ahem. No, I'm not his next of kin, but I have paperwork that states that I have power of attorney. Also, just in keeping with his wishes, I'd like to contact his son, prior to any final decisions being made."

"Certainly, Mr. Wilson. Take as much time as you need. Would you like to have a few moments alone with him?"

"Yes, please."

He walked over to Mr. Barnes' side, gripping his hand while vividly recalling a personal conversation. In Parker's mind, and in Barnes' will, the final mission was clear. What little inheritance was left would go to his distant son, Devin Barnes, and there would be one added measure that even Meg wasn't aware of. Just two months prior, Barnes had asked Parker to become his legal power of attorney, making important decisions about his final arrangements. And, although Parker was mentally prepared to set everything in motion, he hoped maybe for once Barnes' estranged son would be more responsive.

A tear dropped from his face onto the hospital sheets. "Barnes. I can't thank you enough for all you've done. You saw something in me and gave me a chance. Really — you gave me the opportunity of a lifetime. I'll also never forget the way you and your lovely wife, Evelyn, embraced my late wife, Jenna."

He swallowed hard, fighting the golf-ball-like feeling rising in his throat. "Anybody who was kind enough to welcome Jenna will always be a friend to me." He chuckled. "Heck, I'm even convinced her spirit nudged you to sell the B&B to me. If she hadn't, why else would you choose me? I'm nothing but a crazy old house flipper at the end of the day."

Parker brushed a strand of hair to the side, still feeling warmth coming from Barnes' forehead.

"I want you to do me a favor if you don't mind. When you get to heaven, I know you'll be thrilled to see your wife, your mother, and all the loved ones you told me about. But, if you see Jenna, could you please give her a hug for me? Tell her that I miss her and still love her very much."

Parker turned to leave the room but slowed down just before reaching the door. "One more thing. You know that portrait of you and Evelyn? The one you neatly tucked away in the basement. We're hanging it up in your honor, Buddy. You have my word that I plan to run the B&B well and make you proud."

With a final glance at Mr. Barnes resting peacefully, Parker saluted him. "Farewell my friend. Take good care till we meet again."

* * *

In the hallway, Parker ran into Meg, nearly bumping right into her. "Whoa, you made it," he said, while still wiping his face.

She sighed. "Yes, of course. I had to ask Sean to cover the front desk and then I called the car service, getting here as fast as I could. I just heard the news. Babe, I'm so sorry."

He leaned in, giving her a brief peck and a hug. "Thank you."

If Parker were being truthful with himself, he wished she hadn't come. He didn't feel like exposing his emotions, or expressing the depth of his feelings. In fact, he felt numb and just wanted to go home. In his room at the B&B he could spend quiet time with himself and process his next moves for reaching out to Devin. In his room he could simply be alone.

If there was ever a touchy subject that he preferred avoiding, death was the number one contender. It had crept up on him in the past, like a thief, taking what was most precious and dear to him. If death didn't have its way, he'd still be lying in Jenna's arms tonight. There was no question about it in his mind.

To make matters worse — he'd been so distracted by Portia Fennley who looked just like Jenna. There was no mistake that he loved Meg, but the way this woman moved, the color and length of her hair, her mannerisms, the way she smelled. There were a few things that were different, but she was practically a carbon copy of Jenna, making it difficult for him to think straight. Of course, he'd never act on his thoughts and never admit them to Meg. Overall, he was a good guy, but even good guys were subject to weak moments.

He forced a smile. "He's at peace now. That's what matters most."

"I agree," Meg said, gently holding his hands. "But, what about you? Are you okay? I know how close the two of you had become."

Fighting back tears, he responded, "Yes, but what can you do? He was older and sickly. Even if he had a clean bill of health, no one is guaranteed a long life. You just gotta deal with whatever comes your way."

He began walking toward the nurse's station. The urge to hurry up and sign whatever necessary paperwork was welling up inside of him. After leaving the hospital, he'd take Meg home and go back to the B&B to be alone.

She stopped him, this time gripping his arms in place. "Are you sure you're okay?"

"I'll be fine. My head is just swimming right now. I want to make sure I carry out his wishes exactly as he saw fit, that's all."

He felt Meg's soft lips peck his forehead. "And, you will. But promise me you won't put any unnecessary pressure on yourself in the meantime. We have everything under control at the B&B. Even after you left, the guests were very empathetic and supportive."

As not to be insensitive, Parker gave her another hug, pressing her head into his chest. "Thanks for holding the fort down. If you don't mind, let's go ahead and stop by the nurse's station. Then we can get out of here."

* * *

Back in his room, Parker propped his legs up listening to his sister, Savannah, on the other end of the line. The way she explained it, Meg had called alerting her to check on him after sharing the sad news. He didn't mind of course. If anybody understood him it would be his sister. She was there to witness all the pain he'd suffered when Jenna died. She was there to support him through therapy. If anybody understood his state of mind, she would.

"Hey, Sis. It's almost after midnight. What are you doing up so late?"

"I'm up to check on you. I hear that sound in your voice. A sound I haven't heard in a long time. The real question is how are you doing, Parker?"

He closed his eyes, allowing a tear to fall freely. "As good as can be expected. You know how it goes. Times like this always hit home for me. Especially in this case. I kind of saw things ending differently for Barnes."

"I'm sorry, Bud. I know this has to be difficult, but how did you think things were going to end?"

"I don't know. Maybe this was crazy of me to assume, but we discussed him going into a nursing home. I probably envisioned him spending his last days there. I mean, heck Vannah, just yesterday he'd managed to come downstairs and man the front desk for me. It was what we considered to be one of his good days. Imagine if this had happened to him then? If he hurt himself in any way because of me. I would never be able to forgive myself."

"But that didn't happen," she argued. "I'm sure if Barnes were still here, he'd thank you for everything you did. The way you made him feel like he was still the owner of Seaside B&B, even when he'd practically given up everything due to his financial struggles. Then there was the way you consulted him for advice, and honored his legacy by continuing to run the place just as he and his wife did. Not many would do that Parker. You gotta give yourself a little grace."

"Yeah. Grace. Nobody seems to be handing out grace when it comes to losing the people I care about. Where was grace when Jenna was on her last leg? Or where was grace when she was on a ventilator?"

"Parker, you know that's now how it works. We don't always get the happy ending we're hoping for. But, if it weren't for grace, you would've never come out as strong as you did on the other side. Look at you now. You're fulfilling dreams you never knew you had and you're doing it with the woman you love by your side."

He exhaled. "Yep."

"Parkerrr, be honest with me. If you feel like all this is causing you to have a setback, we can easily call Dr. Thompson. All you have to do is say the word."

He raised up and began pacing near the window. Somehow the thought of calling Dr. Thompson seemed so farfetched. He'd done his time, received his therapy and emerged out of his cocoon. Parker fit seamlessly back into what society would consider to be normal a long time ago. He was no longer remaining secluded, sleeping day and night in a dark space while his heart longed to be with Jenna. So, why would therapy be a consideration?

His voice cranked up. "No. I'm fine. We all knew at some point I'd have to get back to normal, including facing life's realities in the future. This was just the first death since Jenna, so it caught me off guard. Thompson prepared me for this. It's just sad, that's all."

"Okay. Just know I'm here for you, as well as mom, dad, and Allison if you ever need us. They've all been asking about you, by the way. I keep trying to explain to them that you're too busy for your own good."

He released a soft chuckle. "I have to reach out to them soon. If not, I know at minimum mom will come knocking at my door."

"You know your mother very well, Parker. She's been dying to see the B&B. But, don't worry, I convinced her to wait until we're done putting our special touch on it, whenever that will be," she teased.

"Don't worry, Sis. I hear you loud and clear. As soon as I finish beefing up the staff in this place, myself, you, and Miguel will start tackling the rest of the property. It's going to be great. I know it will."

A knock on his room door interrupted his train of thought.

"Alright, I can't wait. I'm going stir crazy day in and day out with hubby and the kids. Don't get me wrong. You know I love them dearly, but I can't let all of my design talent go to waste," she explained.

Parker walked to the door barefoot, wearing only a t-shirt and jeans. Every once in a while, the guests had late night requests, but anything past midnight was highly unusual.

Savannah called out on the other end of the line. "Parker, are you still there?"

He turned the knob. "Yep, I'm here. Hold on a sec."

Upon opening the door, he nearly gasped at what he saw. There she was again. Standing on the other side of the threshold, Portia looked every bit as flawless, familiar, and even enticing, but that part he tried not to notice.

"Parker?" Savannah said.

He broke his stare long enough to respond. "Hey, Vannah. I actually have to run. Can I call you back later on this week?"

"Sure, is everything okay?"

"Yeah. Everything is fine —" His voice drifted.

Chapter 8

Frankie and Meg

Drawing in the fresh scent of books was always enough to remind Frankie of her school age days. She was that kid who always yearned for summer reading lists, new school supplies, and a special little reading nook at home. Meg was no different, and now as adults they enjoyed a similar feeling whenever they came out to book club nights.

They listened as the group leader read each word. "Harper became lost in the imagery of stroking her husband Liam's lips. The thought sent chills down her spine, as she recalled the way it used to feel, prior to saying I do. Following their nuptials somehow their passion dwindled down to a minimal exchange of affection and mounting frustration."

Frankie leaned over, whispering to Meg. "I

couldn't do it. If my husband and I were newlyweds and he wasn't all over me, I'd have to address that problem right away."

Raising a brow the group leader said, "Ma'am. Would you care to repeat that for everyone to hear? A lot of women in the group might find your comment to be insightful." She smiled.

"Uhh, sure. I was just saying I think I'd have a hard time with going from a place of being affectionate with my husband to wondering why things changed. Personally, I'd have to speak up and ask him what was going on," Frankie explained.

As the group continued bouncing around ideas Frankie leaned over again, speaking under her breath. "Isn't it funny how we can be so bold and confident when it comes to the characters in a book, but somehow I can't get my love life together to save my life."

Meg's lazer sharp eyes spoke volumes. "What happened?"

"Well, let's see. Should I begin with the part where I definitely made up my mind that I'm ending things with Christian — even though technically he's out of the country, so I guess I'll have to wait. Not that he would care anyway, it's not like we've spoken to each other. Hmm. Or maybe I'll start with the part where a guy I was once engaged to in New York, just moved to the island and is here to stay for good."

Frankie watched as her friend darn near choked

on a mint. Who could blame her? She'd shared an earful that had been brewing inside, just waiting for the right moment to spill over.

Meg raised a finger, whispering back. "What did you just say?"

"You heard me right. I'm no different than the character in this book we're discussing. The issues are plain to see, but actually knowing how to resolve them is another story," she explained, watching as Meg took a sip from her water bottle. "Besides, that's not even the best part. To make things even more complicated, I laid on the beach with my ex-fiancé this week, practically kissing him till the sun came up."

Meg spit water out of her mouth like a sprinkler system that had just malfunctioned.

Stunned at the overwhelming number of eyes staring, Meg gave a slow smile. "I'm so sorry. Water went down the wrong pipe," she explained.

Of course, nobody fell for that line. At least Frankie wasn't. She honestly didn't care who knew about her history anymore. *We all have a past,* she thought. Frankie was tired of lying to herself and hiding part of who she was from others.

As she considered everything, Christian was a nice guy and they'd had a good time together. Some would even describe it as a hot little romance in the beginning. But, for her, the connection had now fizzled into — okay, so maybe she didn't know what to call it. But, a forever love? No way. Not a chance.

Then there was David. She didn't know what to make of their reunion. But she knew one thing. He sent, not just chills, but flames to her core. It felt like more than a superficial crush. This man knew her soul. Or at least he used to, and it definitely felt like something she yearned to have more of.

Once everyone settled back into the discussion, Meg continued whispering. "So, how are you like this character again?"

"I have secrets that I've been harboring and the time is long overdue for me to set them free. It's the only way I can heal. I can't just sit here in this group, pretending to be some sort of overly confident woman, without actually living out my truth. So, I'm starting right here and now. When you and I became friends, I told you I'd been in relationships, most of which turned sour. But David is different. He's back. And to be honest, I don't think I'm over him. We haven't spent much time together, so we'll have to see where this thing goes. But, even if he never re-entered my life, I need to get over this whole 'everyone is out to get me syndrome' or 'everyone will leave me, so I should beat them by leaving them first, syndrome', and all the other syndromes I've adopted over the years. I just need to start being honest with myself and stop suppressing my feelings."

A lady from the group stood up. "Ladies, let me tell you something," she argued. "I'm in my fifties, I've been married for over thirty years, and I definitely consider myself qualified enough to tell you a thing or two about men. There are only two reasons that come to mind as to why this man won't touch her anymore. He's either cheating..."

Another woman in the group snarled. "Oh, here we go. Why does everything always have to be about cheating?" she said.

The first woman closed her eyes, holding up her hand as if she were directing traffic. "Orrr, if he's not cheating, nobody has ever really shown him affection in his household growing up. And, before you argue with me. I know the book said they had passion at first, but it's very possible that's something he learned to express in the bedroom, but has a difficult time expressing it anywhere else." She then took her seat.

Meg nodded. "She has a good point." She then shifted her attention back to Frankie and whispered. "I'm proud of you."

"For what?"

"Forrr being honest with yourself first and foremost. As far as I'm concerned you have nothing to prove to me. I don't care if you told me you were engaged ten times and married twenty. Your past is not for me to judge and your future is not for me to decide."

A warm feeling washed over Frankie, allowing her to feel relieved. "Thank you, Meg."

"Don't thank me, yet. When we get out of here, I still want to hear all the details. We can't be housemates and best friends if we're going around keeping secrets from each other."

Frankie patted her friend on the hand. "Agreed."

"Good. And, in the spirit of being transparent with my housemate and friend, I also have something to confess," Meg whispered.

"I'm all ears."

Frankie glanced over, looking at Meg's face turn three shades of red as she fought to speak.

"I think I'm pregnant."

* * *

Frankie tossed her bag on the couch as Meg followed her in the house. The details of the book club discussion faded, becoming background noise as the words 'I think I'm pregnant' were uttered. The thing about it was, Frankie was all for celebrating such joyous occasions. But, Meg, on the other hand, didn't seem happy.

Frankie arranged a nearby chair, patting the surface. "At times like this I normally like to celebrate, but you haven't been acting like yourself since you told me. What's wrong, Meg? Are you scared?"

An instant flood of tears welled up in Meg's eyes. "Yes, for so many reasons. I feel like I messed up, Frankie. I'm going about this whole thing the wrong way."

"How? People have babies all the time. You'll get through this. Plus, you have Parker, who's an amazing man. What could possibly go wrong?"

"Well, for one, I'm forty-five years old. Forty-five! Do you realize the risk for women my age who've never had a baby? What was I thinking?"

Frankie's face went blank. "Don't you think it would be wise to talk to the doctor about these things before getting yourself all worked up?"

"Mmm. Well, my list of concerns doesn't end there. Do you remember the other day on our walk when we saw Parker with another woman?"

"The blond? Yeah, what about her?"

Frankie hoped Meg wouldn't say the dreaded words. Not the words that often get used when a man decides to stop being faithful. "Please don't say what I think you're going to —"

Meg patted her cheeks, and laughed it off. "No. Not to worry. He wasn't doing anything other than being a gentleman. But —"

Frankie pressed further. "But what?"

"Ever since she arrived, he does seem distracted. That's probably so dumb of me to say. She's a beautiful woman. I'm sure any man would notice her. Besides, that's not even my real problem. We're still in the midst of learning how to navigate the business and our relationship at the same time. In my opinion, the relationship is no longer clearly defined. Some days we're on and everything is good. Other days it's mostly work, work, and more work, allowing everything else to suffer."

Frankie's brows folded. "Everything can't be suffering. You two still managed to find time to make a baby." Regrettably, letting the words slip.

There really was no judgment on Frankie's part. She was the last one to point the finger at anybody. It was just the non-filtered, matter of fact side of her brain kicking in and taking over. "I'm sorry. I didn't mean any harm by what I said. It's just..."

Meg chuckled. "The truth. Trust me, I get it. I have so many mixed emotions running through my head I could scream. This was not the way I planned my life when I was younger. I always thought I'd meet the man of my dreams, get married, and then have as many babies as the law would allow. Okay, maybe not that many, but you know what I mean."

"I do." Frankie smiled.

"Clearly life didn't go according to plan. Somehow it all started spiraling downward the moment I broke off my engagement to John. Another pathetic fiasco in the books."

Frankie tilted her head. "I strongly disagree. That

breakup was the best thing that ever happened, saving you from a multitude of heartache and disappointment. And, it all led you to Parker, and the B&B, and to start a new life that most can only dream of. So, what's your problem again?"

"Don't get me wrong, Frankie. If I'm to be a mother, I'll count my blessings all day, every day. Trust me, I will. I'm just not pleased with how I went about things, that's all."

Frankie stood up. "Am I missing something here? What do you mean if you're pregnant? I'm pretty sure I heard you loud and clear when we were back at the bookstore."

"Well, I'm pretty sure I am. I mean, for the most part, I'm pretty sure. I purchased one of those inexpensive convenience store tests, to hurry up, get it over with and just know. But the lines were a little blurry."

Pacing around the room was Frankie's way of methodically putting the pieces of the puzzle together. There was the B&B which had proven to be taxing on their work schedule, a new blond in town, and a looming suspicion that Parker had no idea that Meg was pregnant.

With reservation Frankie asked, "By any chance does Parker know about this?"

"He doesn't have the slightest clue. And, at this point I have no intention of telling him. Not until I work up the nerve to take another test."

Frankie beamed. "Mmm, and when will that be?"

"Mr. Barnes passed away yesterday, so it's certainly not going to be within the next twenty-four hours."

Observing that her friend was in need of comfort more than anything else, Frankie poured Meg a glass of water. "I'm so sorry for your loss."

"Thanks, Frankie. I spent most of today trying to help out as much as I could, but Parker seems to want to handle everything by himself. He's trying to get a hold of Barnes' son — which is proving to be another difficult situation. I don't know, Frankie."

"How is Parker holding up?"

Meg closed her eyes and exhaled. "It's not like dealing with death is a strong suit for Parker. It's difficult for anybody but I know for certain this struck a nerve, reminding him of Jenna. When I was standing outside the room at the hospital I overheard him talking about her to Mr. Barnes."

Frankie's thoughts wandered, wondering if living a somewhat problem free life was ever really attainable. There wasn't one person she knew that wasn't dealing with some element of struggle as it related to love, death, health, finance — there was always something.

She pushed the glass across the counter. "Here, drink this. And, while you're drinking, I have an idea I'd like to propose."

"I'm all ears," Meg responded, chugging down the first few gulps.

"I think we need a little getaway. It's been way too long. Nothing crazy, but maybe we can catch a ferry over to Atlantis or Baha Mar? Both resorts are so relaxing, plus it will be an excellent way to help you clear your mind. Just for a day or two. What do you say?"

With several strokes, massaging the back of her neck, Meg replied, "While normally I'd jump at the opportunity in a heartbeat, I have Seaside B&B to think about. I can't just leave Parker to fend for himself all day while he tries to focus on Barnes."

Frankie returned to the kitchen, spreading an arrangement of taco shells across a baking pan, then pulled out a container filled with additional fixings. "It's not a long trip, Meg. If there's one thing I'm good at, it's recognizing when you need a break. Now, I want you to call Parker and tell him we'll have you back by Saturday evening to see how things are coming along, but you're taking a few hours for yourself tomorrow, even if it's only for a day. That's it. Girlfriend's orders."

Meg stared, giving the same look she always gave when she realized Frankie wasn't accepting no for an answer. "Okay. I'll agree to this day trip after you introduce me to your new, or shall I say old, friend. What's his name again? David?"

Frankie paused, rubbing her hands on her dish towel. "That's not realistic by tomorrow and you know it."

Meg chuckled. "The same way your idea for a random trip is not realistic, but I'm still willing to go — just at another time. As a matter of fact, I'll make it easy on you. Why don't you extend an invite for him to come along? I want to meet the man you almost walked down the aisle with and see what all the fuss is about."

Frankie's eyes lit up. "We just hung out for one evening. It wasn't even planned. Don't you think it will look kind of crazy to just extend a random invite out of the blue?"

Meg thrusted her pointer finger in the air. "You want to know what looks crazy? I'll tell you what looks crazy. We're two women who desire to have love, but we just can't seem to get it right. You go around dropping men like a bad habit, and yes for some of them, I can see why. But, apparently some of them were really good, Frankie. Me, on the other hand — I do everything backwards before realizing that something isn't right," she argued.

"Backwards?" Frankie asked, noticeably not denying Meg's accusations about her habit of dumping men. It wasn't exactly a reputation she wanted for herself. And she agreed wholeheartedly it was time for change. Of course, that change would have to come right after she respectfully severed ties with Christian.

Speaking of Christian, he must be having a good time abroad since he still hasn't called, she thought.

"Yes, backwards! If I'm carrying Parker's baby, then we'll get through this. We'll make the best of it, I know we will. But I envisioned things so differently in the beginning. I should've weathered the storm in my old position at The Cove instead of storming out of there at the first sign of trouble. Parker and I could've continued dating, and worked on figuring out how to navigate some sort of balance. Then when the time was right, we could've married and ran the B&B together."

Frankie leaned back on the counter. "So, are you sorry you joined him to work at the B&B? You know I can get you another position at The Cove in a heartbeat."

She sighed. "No, not sorry about working at the B&B. I love it there and it's really giving me the opportunity to learn the ownership side of things, which is what I've always wanted. It's just —we're sacrificing our relationship for the sake of the business, and that's not something we had to worry about before I partnered with him."

Frankie watched as her friend struggled, internally wrestling with it all.

"I believe in marriage, Frankie. And, I love Parker

with all my heart, but I'm realizing we should've done this differently, that's all."

"Listen, kiddo. This is just a temporary season you're going through that won't last forever."

"I know." Meg smiled. "I love you, friend. But the two of us have got to figure out how to stop sabotaging our love lives. Seriously."

Frankie walked over, extending her arms opened wide. "I agree. I'm ready to turn over a new leaf starting now. For me, it doesn't matter if a new man ever comes along. What matters is I let go of my fears," she said, giving her friend a hug.

"And, what are those fears again?"

After a snug squeeze and yet another flashback of her childhood, Frankie responded, "My parents' divorce. I lived several years of my life fearful that the same thing would happen to me. So, as a result, I —"

Meg leaned in, interrupting. "You break things off."

Frankie nodded. "Yep. Not just for the sport of it, of course. It's not like I'm a mean person. But, as you said earlier, some of them have been deserving, and maybe other situations could've lasted longer if I didn't run. Either way, it's not like I had any examples of healthy, long-lasting relationships to go by."

Meg grabbed her friend by the hand. "That doesn't matter. It's never too late to change your thinking and the trajectory for your future, right?"

Frankie placed another hand on top of Meg's. "I

can agree to that as long as you're willing to take your own advice."

Meg chuckled. "I will. I'll also agree to our little getaway trip — but, in a little while. Let's first see how things go with —" she said, pointing towards her stomach.

Chapter 9

Meg

Meg inhaled the aroma of Sean's continental breakfast all the way down the hall. He was like a magician, working his magic with sausage and scrambled eggs in a way that was sure to make your mouth water.

In the front, a lady with a pleasant disposition walked through the doors, rolling her luggage behind her.

"Welcome to Seaside B&B." Meg smiled.

"Thank you. I have a reservation under the name Rose Beekman."

"Yes, Ms. Beekman. We're happy to have you. Your timing couldn't be more perfect. Chef Sean is preparing a continental breakfast as we speak."

"Oh, thank you dear. I really appreciate you accommodating my arrival earlier than normal check-in hours. I can't wait to settle in, change into my flip-flops and head down to the beach."

Meg peered outside and then passed her one of the newly designed schedules. "Well, in that case, take this schedule with you so you can get yourself acquainted with the B&B. It has our menu selections on the back. Our continental breakfast is available right now, starting every day at eight." Sliding her finger down the paper Meg continued. "Social hour is between five and six, and desserts prepared by Chef Sean will be out in the dining area by eight. We'll even have some of the finest local wine available if you'd like to indulge. In the meantime, I'll get your key for you. And, if you'd like, you can even sit outside on the terrace while you enjoy your breakfast."

Meg's love for hospitality usually kicked into overdrive whenever she encountered new guests. Meeting people who shared experiences from all over the world was always such a special treat. Chatting with this petite, silver-haired woman with a friendly smile was no exception to the rule.

"Oh, I can tell I'm going to really enjoy myself this week. It's time for some very much needed R&R."

"Well, then please allow me to show you to your room," Meg offered.

* * *

Once Ms. Beekman was settled in the Tropical Paradise suite, Meg slipped into the Blue Lagoon, a vacant room where Parker was fixing a faucet.

She peered around the bathroom door, finding him sprawled under the sink and showing off his manly body. "How's everything going?"

"Given the fact that this sink is about thirty years old, I'd say it's going pretty well. Nothing my wrench and a few other tools can't resolve."

She looked around, observing the array of tools covering the floor. "Have you seen Mr. Fennley at all? I slipped a schedule under his door, but one would think he'd make an appearance to at least eat every now and again."

"Sorry, I forgot to mention it in the midst of all the chaos, but he checked out late last night. Apparently, their troubles in paradise hit the boiling point around midnight."

Feeling shocked, Meg said, "Wow. That was a short stay. Is the Mrs. staying for the remainder of the week?"

Parker grunted, putting all his might into loosening a difficult bolt. "Yep. Last I heard she was thinking about extending her stay, but I'm not sure. In the meantime, I finally caught up with Devin about an hour ago."

Her eyes widened. "Really, what did he have to say?"

"He was guilt-ridden. Apparently, he'd just retired from the service and was planning on reaching out to his dad as soon as he found a place to settle."

Meg held her head down. "That's so sad. Mr. Barnes would've given anything to be able to hear from his son again."

"He sure would've."

"So, what's next? Will he attend Mr. Barnes' funeral?" she asked.

"Not only will he attend, but he's planning all the details." Parker laid his tools down. "Mr. Barnes left specific instructions asking me to be his power of attorney. And, as his power of attorney, one of the first things he wanted me to do was to make contact with his son, giving him an opportunity to get involved first. If my attempt wasn't successful, then I was to handle all the remaining details myself."

"Wow, I didn't realize —" She paused, feeling speechless.

"Yeah. But Devin wants to be present and get some sort of closure I suppose. I'm going to go ahead and honor Barnes' wishes."

Meg wiped a tear. "That's heavy."

"It sure is. But it's what Barnes wanted. And, since I don't even begin to understand the depth of love he had for his long-lost son, I'll be the last one to stand in the way of his wishes. Devin mentioned something about flying him back home to be buried with his mother. Again, it's not my call to make. I'm just glad I had a chance to say my goodbyes," Parker replied.

"Is there anything I can do to help you? Maybe some way we can prepare for Devin's arrival?"

He grunted again. "As I know more, I'll keep you —"

Before he could finish a knock at the door interrupted Meg's train of thought. "Parker, are you in there?" a woman's voice called.

An abrupt opening of the door, followed by Portia Fennley calling out his name was a game changer for Meg. The nerve. And, how did she know he was in there in the first place?

Unfortunately, in an attempt to sit up, Parker banged his forehead, causing it to bleed.

* * *

Meg fumbled through a medical drawer for supplies while Portia grabbed a small towel, filling it with ice. Meg's mind whirred as she rushed feverishly to help Parker, while simultaneously considering how many ways she could kick Portia out.

Surprisingly he seemed agitated with both of them. "Ladies, I'm okay. Really."

Meg paused. Surely, he wasn't referring to both of them? Portia had no business following them down to the main floor for anything. She was a guest at the B&B, not his wife. And, last time Meg checked,

Portia had enough drama of her own to take care instead of coddling over Parker.

Portia motioned toward him. "You have a large knot on your forehead. I'd hardly consider that to be okay. I'm a trained nurse. Have a seat and I'll take care of it in no time."

He glanced at Meg who waved her hand towards the chair. "I'm not a trained nurse but I know how to remove blood and reduce swelling, so the choice is yours. At best you can reach into the drawer behind you and grab some solution and a bandage for your cut."

Parker reached out, pulling the drawer towards him, but paused in the most peculiar manor. He then looked up at Meg.

"What?" she said as her heart sank into her stomach. She'd been so caught up in the moment, completely forgetting about the contents of the drawer.

Parker shifted his gaze toward Portia. "Mrs. Fennley, thank you for offering to help, but I think we have everything under control."

* * *

"Hold on a second. I understand that finding a pregnancy test in the drawer could be cause for alarm, but I'm not the only one who has some explaining to do," Meg argued.

Every ounce of nervousness Meg once harbored

about the test had suddenly dissipated. Observing Portia Fennley burst through the door like she had a personal invitation was more than Meg could handle. Her level of comfort and audacity was enough to send any woman's imagination into a tailspin.

Parker held a bag of ice to his head and spoke calmly. "What do you want me to explain? I'm not the one who bought the test."

Folding her arms, she began pacing. "Clearly. But you might want to explain why you invited Mrs. Fennley to the Blue Lagoon room. She had no business bursting in like that. And, what's all this with her coming to your aid? Is there something going on that I need to know about?"

With a knot the size of a golf ball, Parker put the ice down and picked up the test. "I'm the one who should be asking you that question. If you suspect that you're pregnant, Meg, isn't that something I should know about?"

Meg felt beads of sweat forming in all the wrong places and steam coming out of her scalp. She wanted immediate answers, but instead she took a deep breath. "I recently took a test that had a faulty reading. So, to be certain one way or the other, I stopped by the store on the way in with intentions of getting better results. Typically, you don't go through these drawers regularly, so —"

He nodded. "You figured you could take it without even telling me."

"Come on, Parker. It's not like I didn't try to bring this up with you. I started to say something the other day, but then Mr. Barnes passed. And, ever since then you've been distant. What was I supposed to do?"

He extended his hand with a look of disappointment washing over his face. "You're right. And, I'm sorry. I have been absent-minded as of late."

Meg slipped her palm into his, taking a few steps closer. "Absent-minded is a bit of an understatement, don't you think?"

"I completely agree. But I swear to you, I didn't do anything with Mrs. Fennley," he said, bouncing his head as if weighing the whole ordeal. "If anything, I've been trying to avoid her like the plague.

Meg contemplated for a moment. "Why are you avoiding her and how did she know to come looking for you in the Blue Lagoon suite?"

"I told you she's not one to take no for an answer. Especially when she's looking to vent about her husband or looking for yet another ride into town."

Waving her finger, Meg replied. "Oh, no. That stops today. We're here to ensure she enjoys her stay at the B&B, not to become her therapist and personal assistant."

Parker tugged on her belt loop, drawing her close. "I couldn't agree with you more, but in the meantime, I'd much rather focus on what's important here. If we're about to become parents, there's nothing that would make me happier. Please —" he begged. "Take the test."

Meg wasn't sure what had changed, but the softer, warmer side to Parker had finally resurfaced, once again making her feel like they could do anything together.

"Trust me. No one wants to take this test more than I do. However, Ms. Beekman is here, and I'm expecting her to come down and dine on the terrace at any moment now."

Parker began laughing. "And, I suppose if I go out to greet her with this knot on my head I'll probably scare her away."

"Yeah, you probably should let me handle that."

What Parker didn't know is Meg was already one step ahead of him. She'd excuse herself, go to the restroom, and then carefully place the test in position to check when she got back.

"I can step away and take the test in a matter of minutes. Then in about fifteen minutes or so we can both go in and check. Deal?"

"Are you nervous?" he asked.

"I've been a ball full of nerves since the moment I missed my menstrual. Nevertheless, I'm still standing here holding it together. That has to count for something," she said, looking deeper into his eyes. "You do realize this will change our lives forever — if the test is positive."

"Yes." He stood, wasting no time engulfing her lips.

He then pulled away, lifting her chin. "I realize exactly what it means and I'm ready for it, either way."

Chapter 10

Frankie

Frankie playfully dangled her heels with her toes, wishing she could trade them for sandals. In her mind, even if Meg couldn't make it, she was going to have her one-day getaway sooner than later. She'd been working hard and a break was long overdue.

A buzzing alert from Bree interrupted her train of thought. "Hello, my dear Bree. How can I help you?"

Bree giggled on the other end of the line. "You can help me by taking an important call from Mr. Christian Halstead. He's holding on line two."

"Bree, why do I have this funny feeling you're taking great pleasure in announcing his name?"

"Because you know me very well. Enjoy your call, Boss." She chuckled.

Fighting the unsettling feeling in her stomach, Frankie mashed line two. "Hello?"

"Finally. I was starting to think we may never speak again," Christian teased.

"Actually, I was wondering the same. How are you?"

"I can't complain. This assignment has me wining and dining in some of the finest hotels and restaurants Australia has to offer. It's amazing."

Relief washed over Frankie as she was happy to hear him in such good spirits. She'd quietly hoped their last conversation wouldn't leave a lasting negative impression.

"Australia. Wow, that is amazing. Your boss sure does know how to pick 'em."

"Yeah. There's a team of us on the trip this time. It's been surreal to say the least."

"Good Christian, I'm glad to hear it. You work hard and deserve opportunities like this. I hope the trip turns out to be everything you hoped it would be and more."

The sound of crickets filled the air as she swung around in her swivel chair, observing the grounds of the resort.

Christian broke the silence by asking, "How are things on your end? Hopefully you're not just working twenty-four-seven."

"Well, you know how it goes. Trust me. I'll make time for play soon enough." Glancing at a stack of files, she continued, "Either that or I'll have to take my work with me on vacation. One way or another, a small trip is definitely on the horizon."

"Oh, okay. By any chance would that trip happen to be back to Atlanta anytime soon?"

Frankie could hear a pin drop as she contemplated the appropriate way to break it to him. She envisioned a small trip that involved tropical beverages, beach umbrellas, and perhaps even live music. A little getaway that allowed her to become even more immersed into the culture. Not another hustle and bustle through the airport to deal with the inevitable face-to-face.

A yawn on the other end of the line caught her attention. "It's okay, Frankie. You don't have to pretend anymore. I get it."

"What do you get, Christian?"

"I get that we're not on the same page. And, quite frankly, I don't blame you. Instead, I applaud you for seeing it much earlier than I. You don't want to do long distance, and to be honest, I don't think I'm ready to settle down yet. In the long run, it's actually a win for both of us."

Wait. What? she thought.

She slid to the edge of her seat. "If it's such a win then why did you care to ask if I was coming back to Atlanta?"

"I guess to test the waters one last time. Maybe to see if what I was detecting was really real. Either way, it doesn't really matter. The truth is our differences are far greater than what we have in common, Frankie. My job requires me to travel the world and see many places. In doing so, it's nothing for me to be in a long-distance relationship with someone. As long as it's with the right one, who cares. It's the end goal that matters most. You — well, as I said earlier. We're just on a different page. There's no other way to explain it."

Is he breaking up with me?

She walked over to her bookshelf, glancing at an award she'd won after her second year of working at The Cove. Up until now, her accomplishments gave her the most comfort even when a man couldn't.

"Soooo, where does this leave us?" she asked, intentionally making way for him to bring on the grand finale. She was okay with it. The fact that Christian was ending this this time instead actually gave her great peace.

"It leaves us in a good space. A moment where two adults can be honest with each other with no hard feelings attached. A moment where we can bid each other farewell and hope for the best for each other's lives."

A half smile emerged as she heard the words. "You know what, Christian. Under any other circumstance, a woman would typically be annoyed at a guy who had just dumped her. But, in this case, you did it so eloquently. I can't be mad at that."

He chuckled. "Why, thank you. I'd never considered myself an eloquent breaker upper before — if there really is such a thing."

"I'm telling you, it's definitely a thing." She laughed wholeheartedly, then eased into a long sigh. "Thank you, Christian."

"For what?"

"For having the courage to speak your mind. And, for understanding me. You're an amazing guy, and I know the right one is out there for you," Frankie offered.

"Yeah, yeah. The whole nice guy bit. I've heard it several times before. But you, Frankie Jones. You are truly an amazing woman. And, if I may, I'd like to offer you one piece of advice," he said.

"Oh, no."

Christian chuckled again. "Ha, oh yes! Trust me, it's painless. Or at least it's meant to be helpful, not harmful."

"Okay, I'm all ears."

He waited a minute, then said, "Get out of your own way, Frankie. It's that simple."

She flopped back into her chair, mentally digesting his words.

Get out of my own way.

Looking up, she could see Bree standing beyond the glass, urgently holding a sign that read, 'David is here. He's waiting for you in the front lobby.'

Frankie smiled, then cleared her throat. "You

know what, Christian. That's the best advice anyone has ever given me. I'm wishing you all the best, my friend."

"Likewise. Take care, Frankie."

* * *

Frankie turned her attention to David, the only dark-haired, good-looking man, rising from his seat in the lobby.

"Let me guess. Grant sent you here on another mission?" She smiled. A mission she didn't mind, of course. She was starting to get used to the idea of seeing him.

"Well, kinda, sort of."

Bewildered, she replied, "Okayyy, care to elaborate?"

"In order for you to really understand, you'll have to come with me," he said, lifting his hand toward the front door.

Frankie looked around. "You're kidding, right? I'm in the middle of my work day. I can't just leave."

"Trust me. Grant knows all about it. As a matter of fact, when he learned that we never made it to lunch the other day, he pretty much insisted." He smiled.

"Oh. So we're heading to lunch?"

"It's something like that. Look, do you trust me or not?" he said, extending his hand.

The problem wasn't whether or not she trusted David. That was a no brainer. The real question is whether she trusted herself. She had just endured a break-up. Under normal circumstances her emotions were supposed to be raw — supposed to be being the key objective. However, she'd have to admit the breakup with Christian was anything but normal. It was actually pleasant and welcoming.

Now Frankie was standing before a five-foot-nine familiar heartthrob. A man who knew the depths of her soul, had been dumped by her before, and still longed to spend time with her. This was a lot to digest.

With goosebumps raising on her arms, and a quiver up her spine, she slid her hand in his palm. "I can't imagine what the two of you could be up to, but as long as Grant approves, I guess it's okay."

"Good. Oh, and before I forget —" He turned, reaching for a bag. "You'll need to change into this."

Frankie sifted through the bag removing shorts, a tank top, and flip-flops. Surprisingly everything was her size, causing her to be even more suspicious.

"David Sullivan, you're lying to me and I know it." Her boss had absolutely no clue what size clothing she wore. Plus, he would never do something like this.

Smiling, he fired back. "Look, I may have added my own special touch here and there, but trust me when I tell you Grant is well aware. I can get him on the phone right now if you want me to," he explained while dangling his cell in the air.

"Nevermind. I'll be back," she said, cutting him a look as she resisted the urge to demand details. She then retreated to the restroom to change.

* * *

Frankie observed as David shook hands with a friendly worker by the shore. They talked for a moment, then he reached for the paddles resting beside a kayak made for two.

"Oh, uh-uh. No way," Frankie moaned.

As he handed over a life jacket, he replied, "Come on, I know you're not afraid of kayaking. At least you weren't afraid the last time we braved the Hudson River."

"David, what in the world? This isn't New York. It's almost a decade later, and we're on an island, in the middle of my work day no less. What's gotten into you?" she said, drawing her hands to her hip.

He signaled a thumbs up to the gentleman who'd helped him and began inching closer. "Alright, I should probably come clean and tell you what I've been up to. Grant reached out recently and expressed interest in me taking over the case."

Peering into his eyes, she replied, "As in, take over the case, completely? He's willing to fire our lawyer?"

"Yes, but I respectfully declined. I told him it would likely be a conflict of interest for me to work for his office. Especially given that I have feelings for you."

It was the last set of words that rang over and over in Frankie's mind. "You said that to him?"

"Yes, it slipped out before I could think. But somehow I knew Grant would be understanding. Without going into too many details, I explained that at one time we were more than friends." He chuckled. "The funny thing was Grant detected it all along."

Frankie cracked a smile, exposing her soft dimples. "I don't know whether to be relieved or embarrassed or what." Surely, as the director of HR, there had to be some sort of company policy she was going against. "I should've just been upfront with Grant to begin with."

David nodded in disagreement. "You didn't do anything wrong, Frankie. He was the one nudging me, insisting that I surprise you for lunch and show you a good time. Plus, he's in such good spirits over his new grandbaby, you could practically turn the whole resort upside down and he wouldn't care."

"I don't know about that." She laughed.

"You get what I'm trying to say."

She got it, alright. But still needed a pinch in order to accept the moment as reality. Frankie was still mentally stuck at the airport, somewhere around the precise moment where she turned around, laying eyes on him again.

David extended his hand. "Now that you know the entire chain of events leading up to this moment, I'd love it if you'd join me on a trip down memory lane. Since the water is clear here unlike in New York, I was thinking we could navigate the waves on a kayak for a while, then grab a bite to eat. What do you think?"

Butterflies fluttered at the pit of Frankie's stomach, bringing back a rush of exhilarating feelings. The thrill was still there, and the fire and attraction still blazed between them.

He took her hand, gliding it alongside his beard, the same way he used to when they were younger and in love.

"Alright, let's go for it," she whispered.

* * *

As they paddled in tandem, Frankie soaked in the sun and took in the relaxing sound of the water. She quietly marveled at David's strength, practically taking command of the entire Kayak from behind her.

His deep voice echoed. "Is this bringing back memories for you, the same way it is for me?"

"So many memories. We were so adventurous

back then. We practically did everything in tandem, not just Kayaking," she said.

"Agreed. Even down to our eating habits. I was thinking about the numerous amounts of times we drove upstate just to sit down and enjoy dessert from Pizzeria Unos."

Frankie turned slightly, peering over her shoulder. "It was always the deep-dish brownie sundae that did it for me."

"No, ma'am. It would have to be the Granny Smith All American. It hit the spot ... every ... single ... time."

She flashed back, envisioning his joy as he consumed the dessert, somehow always managing to get ice cream right on the tip of his mustache. He was a kid at heart.

David continued. "How about the time we flew out to Aruba and jet skied across the Caribbean Sea? We managed to squeeze in some memorable times before my career got the best of me."

"We sure did," she replied, gazing over the water.

The two stopped rowing long enough to peacefully glide over the water.

"Can I ask you something?" he said.

The picturesque scene before her with David's voice in the rear was as wild and unimaginable as running into each other after all these years. In one breath she'd landed from Hartsfield Jackson International right back into the presence of the only man she'd ever loved deeply. In her world, opportunities like this didn't exist.

"Ask away."

She could feel him shifting to lean in closer. "If you could do it all over again, would you?"

Trying to suppress the butterflies fluttering out of control, she responded, "David, that's such a loaded question. One that's particularly hard to answer. So much has changed since then."

"I know. For one, you're in a long-distance relationship and all. But I was just wondering. If you had a second chance, knowing what you know now, would a guy like me ever have a shot?"

Frankie whipped her head around. "What do you mean, knowing what I know now? You were consumed with work back then. So much to the point that I believed I wasn't enough for you. Who's to say you still don't have workaholic tendencies?" she teased.

She realized her last comment was probably a stretch, but her issues reached well beyond his work schedule back then. She admittedly was immature and expected that all his time spent away from her must've meant he was indulging in other women. No different than her father did growing up. It was more of a trust issue than anything else.

"You're still holding onto that, aren't you?" he said.

"No. Not really." Turning over a new leaf meant

it was time to relinquish old habits and her old train of thought. David wasn't a villain, and it was time she stopped treating him as such.

He began rowing again. "I uh — I told you one of the reasons I was moving out here was because I fell in love with the island. But, that's not the only reason."

She chuckled out loud. "Let me guess. You looked me up and found me out here, didn't you?" It was a long shot but crazier things have happened.

He laughed. "If I had the slightest clue you were here, I would've moved a long time ago. But, no. That's not the reason."

Again, she peered over her shoulder. "What is the reason, then?"

"I had a near run in with death."

Frankie gasped. "What?"

"Yeah. It was a pretty close call. I stayed at work late one night, burning the midnight oil as usual. I'd say maybe it was myself and maybe two others still left in the office."

Frankie rowed along with him, while carefully listening. "Mm-hmm."

"I can recall glancing at my watch, and deciding it was time to call it quits for the evening. My custom was normally to catch the train all the way up to midtown, but for some odd reason that night I decided to call for a company car instead."

"Mmm," she groaned.

"The driver pulled up in a black Lincoln, I got in, and I don't think we made it two blocks before an ambulance slammed right into us."

Not thinking about it, Frankie turned quickly, almost releasing a paddle into the water. "Oh, dear." As if checking to see if he was okay, she stared at him. "An ambulance?"

"Don't worry. Clearly, I made out okay. I'm sitting here safe and sound as living proof. Although, that day, I was almost certain I wasn't going to make it out of the car alive," he said.

"I'll bet."

"Yeah, it was pretty horrific. The ambulance slammed into our car, clipping the back end behind the driver, sending us into a complete tailspin. If the oncoming hadn't already been at a complete stop that day, only God knows what the outcome would be. As it is, myself and the driver still managed to walk away with glass in our hair, but at least we were able to walk away."

Frankie released a long sigh. "Knowing New York City at night, I'll bet there still was a lot of traffic."

"As always. But, honestly, that's when it hit me like a ton of bricks. I woke up the next morning with a backache and a few minor cuts, but more importantly I woke up with a second chance at life. That's when I made the final decision. No more fast-paced city living, no more chasing pipe dreams of making it big. I knew, without a doubt, I'd put my Nassau license to good use, and I packed my bags to start a new life."

Frankie wondered if all this time, while she was on again and off again in relationships, and struggling with one situation or another, a higher power was really orchestrating what was always meant to be. Had she really spent the last decade of her life just getting in her own way? If so, it had been an exhausting ride and she was finally ready to step aside.

"So, by the time we ran into each other at the airport —"

He interrupted. "I was making my last trip after finalizing a few things in New York. And — now I'm here renting a two-bedroom bungalow, working remotely, and kayaking with you."

His words mixed with the serene tropical setting was enough to make Frankie forget the first part of the day. No breakup, no past remorse could ever take away from the moment. It was way too good — way too surreal.

* * *

Frankie closed her eyes, leaning against the rail of the boardwalk, as David's hands began kneading into her shoulder blades. It was the most intimate moment they'd shared since the other night. She couldn't deny that every stroke he left her yearning for more.

Kayaking and dinner had been amazing, and now she found herself wondering how the evening would end.

"Here we are, yet again, standing underneath another full moon," he said.

"Yes, and if you don't stop massaging my shoulders, I guarantee you I'll fall asleep right here in your arms."

He chuckled. "It wouldn't be the most terrible thing in the world."

A bell rang from a nearby ice cream shop, followed by an announcement.

Quickly opening her eyes, Frankie found her lips to be within inches away from his. "What are we doing, David?" she asked. "Trying to relive the past?"

"I'm not sure. Whatever it is, I think it's something we're both willing to explore."

Frankie wasn't sure her heart could handle any more exploration. She'd already been down that road before, and it left her nowhere — at least nowhere she cared to be.

"And, what makes you so sure I'm willing to explore? After all, I just got dumped this morning. Who's to say you're not a rebound?"

That was probably another stretch of her imagination, since she really didn't have a reputation for being a rebound kind of woman. But still, there wasn't any harm in testing the waters to see how he responded.

"Ouch," he said, standing back. "First of all, whoever this guy was is foolish to walk away from a woman like you. Secondly, I'd hardly call what we share a rebound."

His face shone with a light she hadn't seen before. He was sincere as if he knew exactly what he wanted and how he was going to get it.

"I can't blame it on him. He was just smart enough to recognize where things were heading before me, that's all," she explained.

"So, he broke it off with you, instead of you being the one to break it off with him?"

She laughed aloud. "I guess that's what you call karma. It finally caught up with me. Although, I don't care what anybody says. I wasn't playing games or trying to break the guy's heart. We just weren't a good fit for each other, that's all."

She felt his finger trace along her hairline, tucking a random strand out of the way. "Well, yeah. I could've told you that from the start. You're not the kind of woman to ever build something long-lasting with someone who's miles away. You like the assurance of your man being right there by your side."

Frankie cut him a sharp look, pointing at his chest. "But I took it seriously this time. I really did. I booked flights to visit him and spent time when he visited with me — but I don't know. It just didn't work out in the end. There was no depth there. Just an attraction, which we all know at some point fades away."

Again, she felt the heat of his breath as he inched closer. "And, with us? Did you feel as if we had depth when we were together?"

She leaned in, whispering, "So much that I wanted to have your child, David. In the end, I just didn't think you wanted me in the same way."

His lips engulfed hers even deeper than he did the night before. And, again she was all in, doing everything in her power to keep from wanting more.

He paused, drawing back for a moment. "And, now that you know better?"

Frankie slid her hands up to his collar, pulling him back to her, giving in to every kiss just like it was the last.

Chapter 11

Meg

"It's negative," Meg said, passing the stick to Parker. "Maybe now we can breathe a sigh of relief."

Disappointment washed over his face. "Yeah, I guess." He grazed his hand across her back, giving her a hug. "Are you okay?"

"I have mixed emotions. I've never felt so frightened, relieved, and yet sad all at once. I don't know what to make of it."

Holding her steadily, he said, "It's natural, I suppose."

Meg blinked back the tears forming in her eyes, trying to process everything. Parker had just finished riding his own emotional roller coaster in dealing with a recent loss. And they had other hiccups to sort through as a couple. This unexpected surprise was probably something they should be more cautious about going forward.

She dabbed her eyelids, and perked up. "Hey. We're good, right?"

"Of course."

She knew he was putting on a strong face for her, but wasn't sure if he really meant it.

Meg gathered the box and its contents, disposing of everything in the trash.

"Oh, before I forget, I meant to ask if you'd heard back from Devin?"

Parker reached in his back pocket, pulling out his cell. "Yes, actually. He arrives tomorrow morning. I'll meet him at the hospital to sign off on a few things, and then he's running the show from there. He asked if he could stop by the B&B to gather his dad's belongings and check out the place. I welcomed him too, of course."

The thought of losing a father weighed heavily on Meg's conscience. It reminded her of how important it was to call her dad and check on him, taking time to soak up all the moments she could. Everyone knew the old saying was true; tomorrow is never promised.

"Do you need me to prepare a room for him?" she asked.

"No, it won't be necessary. I can only tell but so much from over the phone, but — it's almost as if he sounds remorseful, while at the same time, determined to get in and get out. It's like he's on some sort of military mission or something. I can't quite explain it."

Meg wiped at her eyes, again suppressing tears. "Wow, okay. Well, this is what Barnes wanted, right? I guess all we can do is honor his wishes. Even though, if you ask me, it all seems very strange."

Parker rested two hands behind his head. "Tell me about it. A part of me wants to go against Barnes' wishes and give him a proper burial, right here in town, not far away from the B&B. This is the place where he and Evelyn last shared their lives together. Not thousands of miles from here, back where Devin grew up."

Meg opened the bathroom door. "Why don't you do it, then? Go ahead and exercise your authority. Barnes trusted you."

"My conscience wouldn't allow it. Barnes trusted me to do exactly what he asked me to. Perhaps he thought if he couldn't get along with his son while he was living, at least they could be reunited in his death. Who knows? One thing's for certain is I'm not going to interfere. Everything is up to Devin to decide."

Meg gazed toward the front porch, where pink Hibiscus flowers adorned the entrance. "Well, whatever you need, you know I'm here to support you."

Gripping her by the hand, "We're here to support

each other. And, this whole thing today with taking the test and all –- it's not over. We need to talk further. We need to ensure that both of us are okay."

"I agree." She smiled. "But, in the meantime, I have a few interviews this afternoon and you need to get rid of that bump on your forehead. Walking around with that thing on your head is sure to get a lot of attention," she teased.

Parker swatted at her backside. "Attention? If that's what you want, I'll give you some attention." He laughed.

"Oh, no you don't. That's exactly what got us in trouble in the first place."

* * *

Highly qualified. Friendly. Excellent references. Meg jotted at the top of the resume. The last candidate for the housekeeping position checked all the boxes on Meg's list. If Parker approved, she'd move ahead on offering the position and free herself to focus on other things.

With their new guests out and about and Portia Fennley still nowhere in sight, Meg eased back to Parker's office.

Bubbling with excitement, she raised her fists to knock on a slightly opened door. But, it was the words that he uttered that caused her to stop.

"Savannah, I didn't touch the woman, I swear.

She came knocking on my door in the middle of the night. Not the other way around."

Meg's heartbeat thumped out of rhythm as she listened to his sister's voice project on speaker phone.

"Well, have a justified reason for knocking? I mean, what on God's green earth could she possibly need from you at midnight?" Savannah asked.

Meg's hand eased down to her side as she stood, listening. Through the crack in the door, she could see the back of Parker's head as he reclined, facing a window.

Sounding aggravated, he replied, "She said she couldn't sleep and figured I was still awake after returning from the hospital. She came to offer her condolences and —"

"Oh, I'll bet she came to offer her condolences, all right. I've got her number," her voice roared.

Parker pressed on. "Vannah, look. I think I handled myself accordingly, like a professional would —"

"I hear the hesitation in your voice, Parker. There's a but coming."

"Yeah, that's the problem, Sis. You know me all too well."

"You might as well come out and say it. You know I won't judge you. Not simply because you're my brother, but because you're a good guy who would never intentionally get himself entangled in the wrong thing."

Meg continued watching through the crack of the door.

"Right. Then you'll understand what I'm about to say. I don't know Portia Fennley, but I'll admit that everything about her reminds me of Jenna. Her hair, her mannerisms, the way she carries herself. Well, everything except for the way she came knocking on my door last night. Jenna would've never been so bold."

"No, she wouldn't," Savannah grunted.

"As I said earlier, I didn't lay a finger on her, although everything about her body language was certainly inviting me to. But Savannah —"

"Yes?"

"I can't sit here and pretend like my mind didn't wonder what it would be like to be with Jenna again. I couldn't help it. It was like something inside of me triggered."

With her stomach in knots, Meg eased away from the door. It all made sense to her now. She'd previously tried to understand why the shift in behavior — why the disconnect and friction between her and Parker. But now that she knew, there was no way to compete. She'd never be a Jenna, or a Portia Fennley. And, if that's where his heart lied, she was even more grateful the test had turned out negative.

* * *

Later that evening, Meg mingled through the guest lounge where desserts and beverages were being served. She inhaled as Sean arranged a display of delectable options, then glanced to the other side where their new arrivals were talking.

Any other day, she'd be pleased to see things running so smoothly. But on this evening, her heart was heavy and her mind was clouded.

From the front foyer, she could hear Parker calling her name. "Meg, do you have a minute? I'd like you to meet Devin Barnes."

Standing at least six feet tall, Devin extended his hand, looking undeniably like Mr. Barnes. From the crease in his forehead, down to his dimples. He even had the same eye color. "It's nice to meet you, Miss."

She gripped his palm, feeling the sturdiness of his handshake. "Welcome to Seaside. Please, call me Meg."

He smiled, then looked around, noticing the picture of his father on the wall. "This is a nice establishment. Looks like the old man has something really special going on here."

Meg glanced at Parker.

"When Devin asked me why his dad was living here, I shared the history of the B&B and all the hard work him and Evelyn put into it," Parker explained.

She nodded.

Devin perused a bit, taking it all in before returning near the front desk. "This is a far cry from the humble beginnings we had growing up. I never thought in a million years my father would move on, leaving us behind to establish something like this."

He shifted addressing Parker directly. "My father must've saw something special in you. I'm glad you were able to plant roots here, keeping his legacy on the island alive. I knew nothing about this part of his life, but I'd like to think he must've chosen you for a reason, so I wish you all the best."

Meg watched as Parker digested his every word, taking it all in. "Can I offer you something to drink? Our guests are gathering in the dining area for a little while. We'd be happy to have Chef Sean whip up something in the kitchen for you."

Devin held out his hand. "No, thank you. I've already put you out of your way by showing up later than expected. I was hoping I could gather my dad's things and head over to the hotel to get a good night's rest. I have to be up and at it bright and early in the morning."

Meg reached into a nearby cabinet, grabbing the key to Mr. Barnes' room. The whole situation was bothersome in her opinion. Where was the closure that everyone needed? She wanted to hear the explanation as to why he'd spent practically his entire adult life ignoring his father. This coupled with the burden of what she knew about Parker was enough to send shockwaves to her head, leaving her on the verge of a migraine.

Devin continued. "I know this has to be awkward for the two of you, so I just want to come right out and thank you for everything in advance. I'm not sure how much my father told you about our relationship, but you reaching out to me, and giving me the opportunity to get involved. It means the world to me."

Meg felt Parker's arm glide over her shoulder as he drew near. "I think I can speak for both of us when I express our disappointment. Neither of us expected that you'd be flying him home."

She noticed Devin's face turning flush. "I have to apologize. It only made sense that he be buried in our family plot back home. It was purchased generations ago, housing some of my ancestors from my great-grandparents on up. I may not have been around to see the life he built for himself here on the island, but the least I can do is give him a proper burial back home."

Relief washed over Meg as she watched the two continue to speak. If they shared nothing else, then at least agreeing to be on one accord over Barnes was more than they could ever ask for. But, truthfully speaking, they did share more. They both shared their love for Mr. Barnes.

"Understood. Would you care to follow me to his room?" Parker motioned.

Portia Fennley entered the foyer just as Parker

escorted Devin upstairs. This time Meg noticed Parker avoiding eye contact altogether.

"Good evening, Mrs. Fennley. Will you be joining us for dessert?"

With tear-filled eyes she nodded. "Please call me Portia. And, no. I won't be having dessert this evening. I need a lot more than dessert to help solve my problems."

"Umm." Meg looked out of the corner of her eye.

"I'm sorry. I know I've already overstepped my boundaries around here. I just need one last favor, if you will."

To proceed with caution would be an understatement for Meg, but a thought that weighed heavy on her mind. She'd already asked for too much, taking what should've been a lovely vacation for two, turning it upside down and disturbing everyone else that surrounded them.

"How can I help you?"

Portia slipped a piece of paper in her hand with a phone number written across it.

"I know this is going to sound foolish. A grown woman like me should be able to take care of her own affairs."

Affairs? Hmm. You mean like the one you attempted to have with Parker when you showed up to his room late at night? Meg thought, but remained attentive. "Mm-hmm."

"I — I was wondering if you would call my husband for me. He's staying at The Cove. Every time I dial his cell phone or his room —" Her voice drifted.

Sparing her the humiliation, Meg offered. "Would you like me to have a friend of mine check to see if he's okay? She works at The Cove and can easily make a call to check on his whereabouts."

"No. I'm sure he's fine. Unfortunately, my husband and I have been down this road before. I was just hoping you'd call and talk to him. If you could ask him to come back here to Seaside, it would mean the world to me."

Meg looked around, peeking in on the guests in the dining area. "You know, I really have to get back to the —"

"Please? I apologize for the way I treated you earlier. I — I guess I just haven't been myself lately. All I can seem to think about is how my husband and I can't seem to get along. He can be so headstrong at times when we disagree. This time I wanted to give him something to think about, but I think I may have taken things too far."

"Do you think?" Meg slipped.

Meg stood there, considering the cost of getting involved.

"Please, Meg. I beg of you. Just one call and if he doesn't pick up, then I won't ask you again."

Meg sighed. "One call. Then I'm returning to the dining area to attend to the other guests. Oh, and one more thing."

"I'll do anything. All you have to do is say the word."

Meg put on the sweetest smile she could muster up. "Keep a healthy distance from Parker. He's already taken."

Chapter 12

Parker

Parker Wilson held a blank stare as he gazed at the moon outside his window. With the day behind him, encompassing a negative pregnancy test, and his meeting with Devin Barnes, the only thing he had strength for was mulling over the day's events in his office.

To make matters worse, he'd only shared a brief moment with Meg, saying their goodbyes as she returned home for the evening. It was yet another thing that was starting to bother him, something that would soon have to change.

He sat, analyzing how much of an impact the last twenty-four hours had on him.

But an abrupt telephone ring gave him a jolt, audibly announcing Savannah as the caller.

Mashing the speaker button, he said. "Hey, Sis."

"There you are. You are the most difficult person to have a full conversation with these days."

"I'm sorry for the interruption earlier. It's been kind of hectic around here as of late."

He stretched his arms, trying his best to snap out of his daze. Savannah was right. It seemed like everything that could go wrong as of late, did go wrong. And, up until now, he'd been going along for the ride, taking in each turn of events as it happened. But tonight, Parker was determined it was time for the tumultuous ride to end.

"I'm glad you called back. I never had a chance to finish my story," he said.

"Oh, trust me. I wasn't going to let you get away with not finishing. What happened?"

"Honestly, I'm starting to realize with all the therapy in the world, there are simply times when I'm going to miss Jenna. It doesn't matter how many years it's been. It's unavoidable and it's just the way things go when death shows up, unexpectedly taking away the one you love. But, make no mistake, I would never and could never cheat on Meg. I love her with every fiber of my being. And that's never going to change."

In the background he could hear his sister clapping, immediately making him laugh. He loved her dearly, but boy she could be a piece of work when she wanted to be.

"Bravo, little bro. Bravo. The only problem is

you're giving this speech to the wrong audience. I'll bet Meg needs to hear your confession way more than I do. Don't you think?"

He smiled. "Yes, but I felt it was important that I clear the air with you as well. You were giving me a hard time at first, questioning my interaction with Portia. And, I just wanted you to know the old family values that mom and dad raised us up with are still live within me today."

Her chuckle quickly dissipated. "All jokes aside. I already knew this about you, Parker. But, every once in a while, I still like to check in and make sure you're still crossing your t's and dotting those i's. Understood?"

He shook his head ever so slightly. "Yes, boss. I understand."

Parker hesitated with the weight of the next subject on his mind, but if there was anyone he could trust to talk about it with, it was Savannah.

"Hey. There's something else I've been meaning to tell you."

"I'm all ears. What's up?" she asked.

He briefly considered how his oldest sister had become his therapist as of late. It was something he was grateful for given the men in his family didn't really talk much to guy friends.

"We took a pregnancy test earlier today, but the results came back negative."

"I'm so sorry. I didn't realize you were trying."

Parker rested the heels of his feet on his ottoman, sinking further into the chair. "We're not, really. If the test had been positive, I undoubtedly would've been a proud father. It was something I always dreamed of back when —"

"I know, Parker," she whispered. "But is that something you would've wanted now, with Meg?"

Still staring toward the moon, he replied, "There's no doubt in my mind. I mean, I know I'm no spring chicken, but as a guy in his mid-forties, I can still keep up with the best of them. We would've been amazing parents."

"I agree."

The truth is this, it had always been his dream to become a father, but the odds were stacked against him and his late wife with her deteriorating health. However, the love he shared with Meg was different. The two women could never be compared, nor would he ever want to compare them.

He continued. "The whole thing was not only a shock, but a total wake-up call for me. Meg was right all along. I've been so caught up in the day-to-day with the B&B, that I've been failing to go out of my way to show her just how much she means to me. Dating but not being fully committed in marriage, and always allowing business matters to come first — or constantly squeezing in occasional quality time in passing, wherever we can fit it in — that's not intentional and it has to end. If not, there will be no us."

"You know what? I'm proud of you, Parker Wilson."

He belted out a loud chuckle. "Why, thank you. I'm so glad you approve."

"No, seriously. You always find a way to work through things, coming out stronger and wiser in the end. It takes some people a lifetime to figure these life lessons out."

"Thanks, Sis. I only wish I had the rest of it figured out." He paused. "In addition to my love life, it's been bothering me that I didn't get to honor Barnes more while he was living. That way he could truly enjoy it. If only I could figure out how to properly honor him the way he truly deserved. He did so much for me. Somehow, just hanging a picture on the wall with a plaque doesn't quite seem to do his legacy justice."

Followed by the sound of clanging dishes in the background, Savannah replied. "I know, bud. In due time an idea will come to you. How's everything going with his arrangements?"

"His son arrived earlier this evening, and picked up his belongings. We had a long talk, which helped me to feel somewhat better about handing over Barnes' affairs. But it's going to take some time for me to get used to our new normal. The place just doesn't feel the same without him."

* * *

Parker's phone buzzed across his desk. He had half a mind to ignore it given the long day, but the annoying urge to see who it was took over, getting the best of him.

Swiping his screen, he saw a message from Meg.

'Parker, I know this is short notice, but I need to take a day to clear my mind. Maybe even two days. Everything is in order and should run like clockwork. No new guest arrivals until next week. -Meg'

He leapt toward his speakerphone to dial her, but his phone went off again.

'No need to call. Spending a day or two off the island to clear my head.'

He shut his eyes, easing back down into his chair.

The idea that Meg would want to suddenly spend time away and not talk to him about it wasn't like her. It didn't make sense.

Perhaps he'd been way more inattentive than he'd thought, missing the little details, pushing her to want time apart.

Chapter 13

Frankie and Meg

"We're going to have to quit meeting up like this. It's starting to become a frequent thing," Frankie teased, strolling alongside David on the blush-tinted sands of Harbour Island.

"That's unfortunate. I was thinking today we could take in the ocean views, maybe grab a little lunch after. And then, I would actually love your opinion on finding one of those cute little coral cottages to purchase, just like the ones over there."

"It sounds like you have the whole day planned out," she said.

"The next two days actually. The cottage hunting might need some additional time."

Frankie Jones sank her toes in the sand, focused on her toes and the vibrant colors of her bathing suit.

She'd do anything to avoid staring at David for too long, not wanting to reveal her innermost feelings.

"I'm sorry. I can't tomorrow. My roommate and I agreed to take a ferry over to Paradise Island. It's our little girlfriend's getaway day if you will. I can't go back on my word."

"I understand. We can still make the most of today, can't we?" He smiled.

"Of course. Hey, you wouldn't believe what song came on when I was driving to work yesterday? I've heard it several times over the past few years, actually."

"Let me guess. Since we're here on the beach, I'm going to go for — Sweet Caroline?"

She swatted at his arm. "Hey, that was too easy. How did you guess?"

"Duh, it was only our all-time favorite anthem whenever we were driving out to Jersey Shore or Jones Beach. What kind of man would I be if I forgot something as important as that?" He chuckled.

Frankie flashed back to not only their times exploring the great outdoors, but so many more adventures, like their irresistible dates at the Lexington Candy Shop on the corner of 83rd and Lexington.

Whipping the hair out of her face, she confessed, "I'll never forget our dates over cheeseburgers and ice cream floats at our favorite corner shop."

David gripped his heart. "Now, those were the good old days. I gained at least two pint sizes after discovering that place, but boy does it bring back memories."

Frankie's face lit up. "Oh, my gosh. Do you remember the time we froze our buns off at the Thanksgiving parade?" She laughed.

"Yeah, but it was all worth it. Waiting for Santa to come at the end and watching him wave to the crowd was like experiencing a real-life childhood dream come true."

As she listened to David reminisce, she realized she was doing it again — falling yet again for another guy. And, although this one had a completely different feel to it, different background and history, *was it actually a good idea?*

"David, I know this is a little random, but — I still have to ask."

"Ask away."

She turned, facing the ocean allowing her hair to blow in the wind. "As I listen to the two of us sharing such wonderful moments together, I can't help but wonder why things went south as fast as they did. I heard everything you said about having to put in the time as a new lawyer at work, and having to prove yourself. I get it. But, if what we had was so solid, I should've been able to see past that and feel confident about us, and I couldn't. Maybe we just didn't know each other as well as we thought. Or maybe we were in love, but we just needed more time."

She glanced at his cheek, then locked eyes with him.

"I'm sorry, but I don't agree. When you're in love like we were— none of that should matter. I believe you had doubts. And, those doubts turned into fears. And, those fears got the best of you, causing you to run." He reached out, touching her arm. "I never thought the day would come where I could say these words — but who would've ever thought in a million years we'd get a second chance. A chance to stay this time, and not run when things get tough."

She watched as he backed off, waving his hands around. "Even if we tried to run, it's not like we could make it very far. We're on an island for God's sake. A beautiful island. And, if you ask me, I think it's a beautiful time to fall in love again," he said, yelling so his voice could echo.

Frankie looked off into the distance. "This is crazy, David. Love doesn't work like this. We've been back in each other's presence, for how long? A little over a week? So much has changed about me since we were together last. I'm not the same woman I once used to be. If anything, I'm probably worse."

David laid in the sand, slowly making angels, as they had done the other evening. "None of that mattered the other night when we were together. We were just two people, freely enjoying one another, making angels in the sand, remember?"

She loved that about him. He was such a free spirit, living unphased or bound by society's norms.

Frankie burst into laughter. "Will you get up? The people out here are going to think something's wrong with you."

"Let them, I don't care." He stood up, dusting off his swimming trunks. "The only thing I care about is not missing another opportunity to be together. I want to love you the way you deserve to be loved, Frankie. That's the only thing that matters to me. The moment I saw you at the airport, I knew that was my chance. My instincts gave me the green light, nudging me to take a chance. What are your instincts telling you, Frankie?"

Nervousness crept up on the inside, causing her to laugh it off. But when she realized just how serious he was, the laughter soon faded. "I don't know. This is a lot to think about. What if things don't work out again? It's kind of like you said — we can't exactly get away from one another."

He slid his hands into his pockets, giving her a slight nod. "That's not quite how I meant it. But, if this is too much, too soon, I would completely understand. It's just — call me crazy but opportunities like this don't normally come along every day."

Frankie felt her heart sink into the pit of her stomach. A strong sense of grief washed over her. She could only imagine the grief stemmed from the years lost, running away from one situation after another.

She could only imagine how different her life would've been if she'd stayed in one place, or in one relationship long enough for it to develop into something more.

David grinned, showing the dimples she adored so much. "Look, I didn't mean to say anything that would shift the atmosphere or bring us down. It's way too much of a beautiful day for that. What do you say we grab a bite, and maybe save the tour of the cottages for another time?"

Frankie sank her feet in the sand as they started walking. "Ok."

* * *

Frankie gripped the strap of her beach bag as her and Meg strolled along the Baha Bay Beach Club.

"Meg, would you look at this place? Between our suite, and this gorgeous view I doubt I'll ever want to leave," Frankie boasted.

"Tell me about it. How did you manage to swing this reservation again?"

Frankie waved, pointing out the perfect spot to claim a couple of lounge chairs. "I used my employee perks. They offered two days, with full access to the East side of the Grand Hyatt, including the beach and the water park. If this doesn't help us relax and clear our minds, I don't know what will," she said, nudging Meg. "Glad to see you taking me up on my offer, by the way. As much as I begged, I still didn't think you'd actually take time off from the B&B."

Meg laid her bags down and began removing her cover-up. "Neither did I, but something had to give, Frankie. I can only take but so much without feeling like I'm about to explode."

Cutting a sharp look, Frankie replied, "Okay, we really need to talk then. I couldn't get you to budge during the ferry ride over here, but it's pretty obvious you need to let loose. What's going on? I'm assuming you got the test results back."

Meg locked eyes. "Negative."

"Negative, as in —"

She continued. "I'm not pregnant, but I certainly have enough drama going on to make up for it," she explained.

Frankie slipped out of her sandals and reclined her lounge chair just so. "I'm sorry. I'm sure the results had to be a little disappointing even if you weren't planning on having a child." Frankie imagined for a moment what it would be like to feel life growing on the inside of her body, or even to see the look on her mate's face in reaction to the news. It was something she knew she'd never experience.

"Thanks, but we'll be okay. At least, I think we will. Parker seemed disappointed at the news, but then again, it's pretty hard to read him these days. One minute he's one way, then the next I don't even recognize him. That's why I decided to take some time for myself. I needed to cool down and get my act together before I said something I'd later regret."

Frankie's eyes widened. "Like what?"

"For the first time in my entire career working in hospitality, I had to, air quote, kindly threaten a guest to stay away from my man. That's not me, Frankie. I don't normally behave like that."

Perking up, Frankie responded, "You? Nooo."

"Oh, yes! I'd had enough of Portia Fennley flaunting herself around the B&B. She acted as if she was ready to devour Parker, like he was a piece of meat. I'm sorry, but where I'm from, we don't put up with that nonsense. I know she's going through some things, but it's not acceptable."

"Agreed. I wouldn't put up with it either. But, what did Parker have to say about it?"

Flopping her hands in the air, Meg said, "I don't know. I never had a chance to ask him. But I did have a chance to overhear him talking on the phone with his sister about how Fennley reminds him of Jenna, his late wife. Oh, and how every time he sees her his mind starts to wander. Something ridiculous like that."

Frankie's mouth dropped. "Nooo."

"I really need you to come up with another response other than no, Frankie. The situation is already bad enough," she snarled.

Frankie felt terrible for Meg, but it just didn't sound like something Parker would say. He'd always been an upstanding, honorable kind of guy. The kind of guy any woman would dream of having by their side. Of course, maybe that was the problem.

"Sorry. But, are you sure you heard him, right? Eavesdropping never works in your favor. I should know, as I've been guilty of doing it a time or two."

Meg feverishly rubbed sunscreen down her leg. "Was I wrong for listening in? Yes. Do I care at this point? No. I'm not going to have my time wasted by anybody, under any circumstance. If Parker can be so easily swayed, then to heck with it. We shouldn't be together anyway."

Frankie sighed. "Oh, boy. We should probably order a couple of drinks."

* * *

Later that evening Frankie pushed the doors open to the private screening room in their suite. She had an appreciation for the career she'd built and the connections made at The Cove resort. All of it afforded her opportunities for her to travel and enjoy their amenities.

"Meg, would you look at this? Our own private screening room to watch movies. We may have just died and gone to heaven."

"You're nuts, Frankie." She laughed. "But I'm grateful you thought to extend an invitation to me. I'm just sorry you didn't bring your new lover boy along so I could meet him. I'm sorry, I guess I should be referring to him as your old lover boy."

A frown washed over Frankie's dimples. "We should probably refrain from talking about my love life or lack thereof. I don't have a lover boy now, and I doubt I ever will. You on the other hand need to tell me what your plan is for approaching Parker. You can't keep skating around the topic forever."

Meg flopped into the plush seating in front of the big screen. "First of all, we're not refraining from talking about anything. Let's face it, that's why we're here. When a woman says she's going away with her girlfriend to clear her mind, she really means she's going to vent about everything going wrong in her life with hopes that she can return back home and fix it."

"True."

Meg pointed. "Good. Now that we're on the same page, we also didn't come here to retire early for the evening or sit in this luxurious movie room. Let's take a walk downstairs while we talk. Maybe even pass through the casino along the way."

* * *

Goosebumps prickled her arms as Frankie perused alongside Meg through the casino. She watched as a group gathered around the card table, cheering one winner on. She then glanced at a sweet older lady as she pulled the lever on a slot machine, shouting aloud for a big win. All the while, her mind drifted back to David.

"Meg?"

"Yes?"

"Is it crazy of me to be curious about seeing David again? To wonder if things could be better a second time around?"

She felt Meg's hand tug on her shoulder. "No, if that's where your heart is leading you. What would make you think that?"

"Guilt maybe," Frankie explained, pausing to stick a bill in a slot machine of her own. "A part of me wants to see him again. The other part of me wonders if I shouldn't just take the rest of this year off and not date at all. Maybe hit the reset button and stay clear of trouble, if you will. It's not like the call with Christian didn't just happen less than seventy-two hours ago."

Meg begged. "And? Please tell me you're not going to allow that to get in the way."

Shrugging her shoulders, Frankie replied, "I might. I have to start gaining some form of control over this part of my life, right? If not now, then when?"

Jarred by the way Meg gripped her shoulders, Frankie stopped fiddling with the machine.

"Frankie Jones, I want you to listen to me. You're not going to gain control of anything by just letting life have its way with you all the time. You need to take better control of the reins. Start making decisions that will lead you in the direction you want to go," she said, sucking in air. "Oh, and one more thing — those decisions can't involve you running. If it's David you have feelings for then don't just dip your toes ever so slightly in the pool and expect good results. Get on the diving board and dive all the way in, for goodness' sake. See how things go. Don't be afraid to get a little —"

Frankie interrupted with a chuckle. "I get it. Please, no more analogies. I get it."

Noticing the sweet lady from the slot machine popping peanuts in her mouth, one by one, while she listened. Frankie smiled. She couldn't blame her for listening in. They'd made quite the spectacle of themselves, standing in the middle of the machines, revealing her love life to the public.

Frankie hesitated. "So taking some time off would probably be —"

"Completely out of the question," Meg bellowed. "Don't get me wrong, there's certainly a time and place for it, but this is different, Frankie. Not only do you two have a history together, but here you are again — on the same island. To me, that's so rare. If you really still have feelings for him, I wouldn't blow it."

Frankie tried to envision how she would initiate contact with him again. Would she call? Would she wait to just run into him? They'd certainly shared a nice morning together, but they'd parted ways without her ever really addressing the matters of his heart.

For all she knew, maybe he'd lose interest.

"I'll do it. I don't know how, but I know I can't go on, ignoring the way he makes me feel forever. So — I'll take a leap of faith. I'll come right out and tell him that I'm interested. What's the worst that can happen?" Frankie confessed. To her left she noticed the same sweet lady holding her hands together in a prayer pose with a grin smeared across her face.

Meg smiled, then spoke in a low tone. "Good. Now, unless you want to attract more onlookers, go ahead and play a few rounds so we can get out of this place."

* * *

Frankie pierced a fork into her eggs Benedict while soaking in the grand views from Café Madeleine. One could've easily mistaken her for a tourist if her I.D. didn't prove otherwise. Meg, on the other hand, dabbled with her breakfast seemingly preoccupied.

"I figured this morning we could get a massage, then head back to the beach to lay out to sunbathe for a while before catching the ferry."

"Sure. I'll follow your lead."

Frankie observed as she bit into her bacon, half-heartedly paying attention to the rest of her food.

"Have you made any decisions about what you'll say to Parker when we get back?"

"No. How could I? I spent most of the night reading one text message after the other, of him looking for reassurance that I was okay. I barely got any rest last night."

"Aww, Meg. He's just being his attentive self, that's all. Parker's smart enough to sense something isn't right. You may as well get right down to it by having the conversation when you get back," Frankie responded, patting her friend on the hand.

"And, say what? Where do I begin, Frankie? 'Hey Parker, thanks for the good times we've had to-gether, but since I'm not pregnant and since you'd rather be with a woman who reminds you of Jenna, I'll just be on my way now.'"

Frankie leaned back, sipping from her coffee mug. "Oh, geez. You know that's not the case, Meg. Come on."

"Really? Do I?"

Frankie pushed up from the table and stood tall. "That does it."

"What are you doing?" Meg said. "Sit down."

"No. I will not sit down until you listen to what I have to say and swear you'll follow through on every word. Now, last night you preached a whole sermon to me about making decisions that will take me in the direction where I want to go. That was you, wasn't it?"

Meg looked around, slowly beginning to sink in her seat. "Yes."

Frankie was comfortable in her skin putting on a full performance if it meant saving her friend's relationship. It was just like they said at their book club meeting — they had all the confidence in the world when it came to judging the character in the story, but when it came to their own lives, that was another ball game.

"Now. You will get up from this table determined to lay a few ground rules if Parker wants to continue to be with you. Are you listening?" she asked, trying to keep a straight face.

"Yes."

Frankie continued. "Good. Ground rule number one. If he wants to continue to be with you then he needs to do two important things. Keep your relationship first, above all else. And, he really needs to propose. Let him know that although you guys had a close call, you're a traditionalist at heart, and you don't want to play house with him."

Meg peered from under her visor. "Okay."

"And, while you're at it, let him know you're more than willing to support him when dealing with loss. But, if you're going to be the only woman in his life, then he truly has to make you the only woman in his life."

"Well, I really don't think he'd ever cheat, Frankie. It's just —"

"Eh eh. I know he's not a cheater, but emotionally he was allowing his mind to go places it shouldn't. And, in your defense, no woman wants to be made to feel like her man is struggling emotionally over another woman." She then mumbled, "Even though, you wouldn't have known about any of it if you hadn't been eavesdropping." Frankie winked.

She could tell by the way Meg began easing upward that she was coming around to the idea. Sometimes she had to go the extra mile to get her point across with Meg, which was fine because Meg always did the same for her. *Whatever it takes,* she thought.

"Okay. I get the point already. How about we finish our food and carry this conversation outside where there's much less of an audience?" Meg begged.

"You get the point, but will you do it?"

Meg confidently positioned her shoulders upright and put her fork down. "Okayyy, Frankie. I will have the discussion with him when we get back tonight."

Chapter 14

Meg

Meg stared at the sign on the front that read 'Seaside B&B' for what seemed like five full minutes. Somehow with the tropical moon shining so bright it looked a little different. Perhaps it was the driftwood frame or maybe it was something else; she wasn't really sure.

Either way, standing outside and staring at the picturesque scene was far more enticing than admitting everything she had to say to Parker.

The sound of a door creaking changed everything.

Parker stood, leaning on the frame. With his hands positioned in his pockets he said, "I was so happy to see your message from earlier, stating that you were coming home today. But, from the looks of things, you're not happy to be here."

Meg chuckled ever so slightly. "Home?" Holding her purse in front of her, she said, "This is not home for me, Parker. It's just a place where I check in by a certain hour and check out at the end of the day. A place where I've dedicated a lot of my time, but don't seem to be getting much in return for it. It's a lot of things, but it's certainly not my home."

She watched him approach her almost turning pale. "This place is just as much mine as it is yours. Meg, please. Tell me what's really bothering you and I'll do anything to fix it."

Meg drew in a deep breath, failing to make eye contact. "Where do I begin?"

"I know you said I wasn't being attentive enough. And, I've already made up my mind that stops today. As in, right now. No excuses. We always come first going forward and not the business," he pleaded.

"Parker, there's more to it than that."

He bent slightly, trying to align his eyes with Meg's. "Okay. Tell me. What else do you need me to change? I'd do anything for you."

She heard the words, but wondered if his emotional ties were so deeply embedded that he couldn't see it for himself. She once heard the soul ties shared with a lover could be so strong that it could last a lifetime. Would that potentially be the case with him and Jenna?

"Sometimes there are things that stretch far beyond our control. Things we couldn't change no matter how hard we try."

His eyebrows folded. "Like what?"

"Like the bond you had with your late wife, Parker. A bond so strong, it's causing you to search for traces of her in other women. Particularly women like Portia Fennley."

He looked winded at first, but then cupped his face inside of his hands. "I messed up."

"I knew it. I knew it all along. It was just like you told your sister. You were starting to have feelings for her, weren't you?"

He tilted his head, seeming confused. Then he professed. "I'm not sure what you overheard, but what I told my sister is there were things about Portia that reminded me of Jenna. That part, I won't deny. They look alike, even carry themselves alike to a certain degree, except for all the forward and demanding behavior," he said, laughing it off. "But that doesn't change anything in here for me," he said, pointing to his heart. "The only woman I want in my life is you. Savannah knows it. I know it. The only person I've been doing a terrible job communicating that to is you."

"Then why did you just say you messed up?" she asked.

"Because that conversation I was having with Savannah, which clearly you overheard — it should've been with you. I messed up big time and I'm sorry for that."

If there were ever a time where she felt relieved, yet frustrated, it was now. She'd planned the way the entire conversation would go, not taking into account he'd have all the reasonable responses.

Staring off at the sign again, she asked, "Well, how do you explain what you said to Barnes that night at the hospital during your final goodbye?"

A smile larger than life appeared on Parker's face. "I don't know, but I'll tell you one thing. I better watch what I say around you, woman," he teased.

She loosened up, swinging her purse at him. "What are you trying to imply?"

"Nothing, my dear. Nothing at all. I would imagine you're speaking about the part where I asked him to tell her I love her, right?"

Feeling foolish, Meg ran her hand through her hair and began pacing. "And, that's perfectly normal. I get it. You lost the love of your life."

"Years ago. And, since then I've moved on to you."

"I know," she stated.

"Do you?"

"Yes. But you have to know I'm not just making this stuff up out of thin air. You played a role in aiding my insecurities. Should another Portia come along, or any other situation that triggers your deep love for Jenna, I need you to communicate with me.

At least let me know what's going on in your mind so I don't have to wonder. That, plus the timing of the test. It was too much."

He reached out, cupping the side of her cheek in his hand. "So much that I pushed you away, causing you to not want to be around me. I'm sorry, Meg. You have my word, that will never happen again. Sometimes us men, we can be stubborn. Keeping so much bottled up inside or running to select people in our lives to find comfort. In this case the only one I should've been running to is you."

Her head folded into his chest as he held her from behind. This was the man she knew from the depths of her soul. This was the man who she'd fallen so deeply in love with before everything came crashing down.

"And, Parker. There's one more thing," she spoke softly in his ear.

"What is it, babe?"

Meg could hear Frankie's voice playing over like a recording, rehearsing line by line what she should say. But, the real question — did she feel all those things in her heart?

"I'm not okay with us getting pregnant before we establish —"

She felt a touch from his finger over her lips. "Before we establish our bond as husband and wife?"

Meg peered into his eyes, this time feeling relieved and very much understood. "Mm-hmm. That and I'm not exactly twenty-five anymore. We may need to reconsider a few things."

Parker eased his hand around her waist. "I'll follow your lead. We can adopt children someday, giving them a loving home or spend the rest of our lives chasing one adventure after the other together. Either way, you have my full support. But, right now the only thing I want to consider at this moment is the surprise I have waiting for you inside." He smiled, then motioned his hand toward the front door. "That's if you'll join me of course."

A feeling came over Meg, causing her to flash back to the moment John, her ex-fiancé, was preparing to propose. It was nothing short of a grand performance orchestrated to appease everyone else but those that mattered most. It was what you did back then when you were born and bred from wealth. And, to think, she was so madly in love with the idea he'd finally proposed, she went along with it. Even if in the end it was a mistake.

This time, she was with the man she was supposed to be with. She was certain of it now. She only hoped that her act of taking time away helped him have an awakening, realizing how important their relationship truly was.

* * *

Parker Wilson signaled to Ms. Beekman who sat in what some would consider a modern-day parlor room of the beach house. In fact, she rested in one of Barnes' favorite corner chairs while peacefully playing the harmonica.

Meg stood still in the entryway, noticing a lit candle covering practically every corner of the room. She gasped, holding her chest. "This is so beautiful. You did this all for me?"

She laid down her purse, then looped her arm around his. "Since when did we start hiring our guests to help execute romantic gestures?" She smiled.

"When a man upsets the love of his life, nearly running her off the island, he'll do anything in his power to make it right. If that means going to great lengths, and accepting the services of Ms. Beekman who generously offered. I'd gladly do it all," he said, facing Meg. "But before I go any further, I have a very important question to ask you."

With her heart racing as fast as it was, Meg was certain she'd pass out. Whatever it was he wanted to say he'd have to hurry up and say it before she ended up on the floor.

"What's that?"

He signaled Ms. Beekman who played another tune. This one was even more lovely than the first.

Parker cleared his throat. "As you know, this is the room where Barnes sat me down and changed my life forever. Until meeting him I thought I'd spend a lifetime going from house to house, remodeling, and selling. At least I thought that's the only thing I'd do. But it was right in this room that he offered me the deal of a lifetime, allowing me to buy the B&B well below market rate."

"Mm-hmm," she said, with an adrenaline rush running through her veins.

"This was also the room where he entrusted me, making me the executor of his will, and trusting me to carry out his mission to reconnect with his son."

"Right."

He turned, reaching for an envelope tucked away in a bookshelf. "Well, now it's my turn to pass the baton. You've been right here by my side, proving yourself to be so much more than just my manager. You've always been much more to me, but I need you to read this."

Meg took the envelope, folding her brows as she reached inside. It wasn't quite the proposal she was suspecting, but he definitely had her attention.

Her eyes quickly scanned line by line when it all started to make sense. "You're making me an equal owner in the B&B?" she asked.

"Why wouldn't I? You're here night and day, putting in sweat equity, and learning this entire business from the ground up just like I am. We're in this together just like we've always been from the start." He held his arms up, in surrender. "Now, don't mistake what I'm trying to suggest here. Our love still comes first. I don't ever want to make that mistake again. But all you have to do is say the word and you and I both will be listed as the official owners — together."

By this point Meg's heart and mind were racing at the same time, one trying to outdo the other. Her mind flashed, envisioning herself as a proud owner like she always dreamed she would be someday, then reality began setting in, deflating her dreams.

"There has to be a catch, Parker. Most people would never do something as drastic as this without expecting some sort of investment. And, you already know that I don't have much to go around."

Parker signaled Ms. Beekman one more time, triggering her to ease out of her chair. "It's been my pleasure to play for you this evening. God's blessings upon the love birds now and always," she said, bowing her head, and then disappeared.

Parker lightly grazed his hands down the side of her arms. "You already made your investment in me the minute you gave up everything to join me here. Isn't that enough?"

"Well," she stumbled.

"Besides, imagine if Barnes had the same kind of mentality. I wouldn't be here today. The least I can do is extend the same to my future wife."

Her eyes darted downward, noticing the way his hands were trembling.

"Meg?"

She looked into his eyes. "Yes," she whispered.

"This setup tonight, it's not much. And this ring —"

Her eyes followed the motion of his hands, reaching into his back pocket, then bowing down on one knee. "Well, it's the best ring I could find at the local jeweler. But this ring, this business, and every other material thing the world has to offer means nothing without you. Absolutely nothing." He opened the box, revealing a beautiful sparkling diamond. "Meg, the only thing that matters to me is you — will you marry me?"

Chapter 15

Frankie

Frankie Jones paced to one side of her office, darn near furious at herself. "I deserve to be happy. Who cares that I messed up in the past? That's why they call it a past for goodness' sake." Her hands flailed.

Pacing around and talking to herself wasn't exactly the sanest thing she'd done all day, but sometimes love made her do crazy things. Fortunately, Bree busted in, bringing an abrupt halt to the madness. She tilted her head. "You okay, Boss?"

"I've seen better days. Just letting my frustrations get the best of me, that's all," Frankie explained.

Bree dropped a stack of files on Frankie's desk. "I hear ya. Speaking of frustrations, I have some news that's not going to sit too well with you. It's not going to sit well with Grant either."

Meg rolled her eyes. "Oh goodness, what now?"

She laid a letter on top of the files, pointing toward the letterhead. "Looks like Lawson and Lawson is dropping us as a client. We have a case to deal with in a matter of weeks with no labor attorney to represent us.

Meg leaned over, meticulously combing through every word. "No. That can't be. Even if our lawyer isn't able to handle the case, surely somebody from the firm can take over."

"Sorry, Boss. I called to confirm before bringing you the bad news. Turns out the entire firm is going under. Apparently, the finances aren't what they used to be. Their secretary explained they've been seeing a steady decline over the last two years forcing their big boss into retirement."

"This is so unprofessional. Surely they could've given us a heads up."

Frankie slid a pen through her bun, trying her best to figure out how Grant would want to respond. It had always been in her blood as a business woman to be two steps ahead at all times, with a game plan, ready to throw into action at a moment's notice. She was the director of HR, but Grant treated her like a right-hand man in a lot of ways and she wasn't about to let him down now.

Her eyes widened. "Bree, I need you to reach out to every top tier resort on the island. Well, for clarification, it's not like there's many, but still. Call them one-by-one and explain whose office you're calling from. Ask if they would be kind enough to offer a recommendation for a labor attorney. If that doesn't work, we're going to have to expand our wings and look beyond the island.

"Uh, okay. Sure, if that's what you really want," Bree responded, and shrugged.

Frankie knew the suggestive tone in her assistant's voice. She could detect it better than anyone.

"What's the problem, Bree? According to this letter we need a new lawyer like — pronto. Winning this case has to be a no fail mission, remember? It's difficult enough dealing with a former employee who wants to falsify information about an injury, but a lawsuit is not a good look for the resort. We need to nip this in the bud and we stand a great chance at doing so, especially since we have proof."

Bree pulled out a chair, making herself comfortable. "Boss. I don't mean any harm by what I'm about to say, but sometimes you have a difficult time seeing what's right in front of you." She smiled.

Frankie sighed. "Grant is going to be back in a matter of days. It's bad enough I have to call him while he's supposed to be enjoying his family. What am I missing here?"

A grin about a mile wide stretched across Bree's face as she sat back, crossing one leg over the other. "Drum roll, please."

Frankie waited.

"I have two words for you. David Sullivan. Why don't we call him up and ask if he's available to take the case?"

Putting her hand up, Frankie refused. "No. No way. He's trying to get settled in to his new life here on the island. The kind of representation we need calls for a more rigorous schedule over the next few weeks, and from what I gathered that may not be what he's looking for."

"Frankie, come on. Don't you think it might be better to give him a chance and ask him first?" Bree said, swinging her pointer finger. "Besides, it could also be another chance for you two to finish what you started."

"Bree!"

Playing innocent like she had no idea why Bree would say such a thing was a defense mechanism for sure. But, in reality, the mere mention of David's name was enough to make her blood rush straight to her head.

"Don't Bree me. We've been working together long enough to know each other way better than you give me credit for. I mean, come on. If you caught me in a near passionate kiss with one of the hottest guys on the island, would you encourage me to finish what I started?"

Frankie paused the pacing long enough to ask. "You think he's hot?"

Bree pointed again. "See, I knew it. Look at the

way you just turned three shades of red at the mere mention of him."

Frankie rolled her eyes. "This is ridiculous. We're getting off track."

"No, we're not. We're onto something very good here. Putting your feelings for each other aside for a moment, Grant's the one who chose David, which means he has a high regard for the level of work he does. All we have to do is talk to David, and see if we can secure him for the job. It doesn't have to be an indefinite thing. After the case is over, he can go back to resuming his normal schedule, and we can search for someone to work with on a more permanent basis. What do you think?"

Frankie peered inside the files, agreeing they needed to act fast. But, was David the right fit? Or was this only a surefire way to immerse herself smack dab in the middle of trouble?

Massaging the crown of her head she said, "Let me reach out to Grant first. This is a big decision, and while I agree that Grant is probably going to want David for the case, let him have the final say, not us."

"Of course."

* * *

Later that evening, the touch of his firm hands kneading into her shoulders was enough to give Frankie the chills. David had this particular way of moving in circular motions, giving her the best back rubs she'd ever had. While he applied just enough pressure, she wished the moment would never end.

His smooth voice soothed her. "Now that we're back together, I can spoil you like this all the time," he said.

He didn't have to say it twice. It felt so good he could give her massages until his hands fell off and even then — it still wouldn't be enough. "David, where have you been all my life?" she asked.

He nestled his cheek beside hers from behind, while gently wrapping his arms around her waist. "In the concrete jungle of midtown Manhattan, waiting for you to come back to me," he whispered.

Frankie slid her arms on top of his, returning the affection. "You weren't exactly spending all your time waiting for me. Even you admit to getting engaged, remember?"

"Touché. Touché. But I was never as happy as I am now."

She whipped around, looking straight into his eyes. "How did you know, David? How did you know I was the one for you back then? And, how do you know I'm the one for you now?"

He traced his finger around the tip of her nose. "You were and still are the only woman I could ever use the word forever with. It's that simple. Despite me moving on at some point and getting engaged, I was never able to carry things through with her. But

— you. You and I had a whirlwind of a romance with the potential of a lifetime of love. It was a forever thing and I've yet to meet anyone else who could ever fill those shoes. I'm sorry it ended, but I'm not sorry we're here now, ready to start over again."

In the background, the annoying sound of the doorbell ringing snapped Frankie out of a deep sleep. She stared for what felt like an eternity at the ceiling fan above her, then looked at the clock. That's when she realized she'd been dreaming.

Darn it! It was just getting to the good part, she thought, while still cradling her pillow. That's the way it always worked with Frankie's good dreams. Whenever it felt that real and that good, the dream always left her hanging, and wanting more.

The doorbell rang again.

"Meg, are you still here?" she shouted. Although, she knew it was highly unlikely as Meg was an early riser.

The doorbell rang again.

Frankie swung her covers to the side, angrily scooting to the end of the bed to find her slippers. Whoever it was, it better be really good to get her out of the bed this early, during her work from home day no less.

"I'm coming," she shouted.

She didn't care. Striped pj's, messy hair and all. If someone was going to have the audacity to ring her bell this early, they deserved all the morning breath and messy hair she could conjure up. Especially if it was the local delivery guy. He had a crush on Meg so bad it was obvious for the whole neighborhood to see. She didn't know how many times she'd asked him politely to just leave her packages on the front porch, but with a big grin, he still rang the bell every single time.

Angrily flipping the locks over, she swung the door open while stating, "All you have to do is leave the boxes right here on —" She paused.

The mailman never looked so good, she thought. Of course, that's probably because it wasn't the mailman, but instead it was literally the man of her dreams, standing right in front of her.

"David?" she said, feeling instant embarrassment over her messy hair, don't care, attitude.

He suppressed a smile. "I'm sorry. I found out from Bree that you were working from home today, and she said it would probably be a good thing to head over first thing and talk. But — if this is a bad time."

I am going to wring Bree's neck!

"No." She looked down, smoothing out her stripes. "Well, maybe. I haven't exactly had my first cup of coffee yet as you probably can tell. And, uh. I can't imagine why Bree would send you over to my house. A conference call would've been the more likely route. At least whenever I'm teleworking."

He nodded. "Yeah, well it wasn't entirely her

fault. I received a call from Grant late last night. We had a long talk and after much back and forth, he convinced me to take the case."

Frankie folded her arms, suddenly forgetting about her physical appearance. She knew he was after a freer and more independent lifestyle here on the island, and she understood why. But, why should Grant have to twist his arm over it? One would think he'd be grateful for the generous check that would come along with the job if he wanted it, plus the independence to still work from home, and most important of all, the access to her. Okay, maybe the last part was a stretch, but still.

"First of all, I highly doubt Grant sent you here this early in the morning. And, why all the back and forth over the position? This is easy money for someone like you, but if you don't want it all you have to do is —"

He stopped her. "It's not that I don't want the job, Frankie. Clearly, I accepted his offer. But I have to be honest. I did toil with the idea of being around you."

She squinted her eyes, wishing she could return to the pleasantries of her dream. It was certainly a lot more palatable than her reality. "Oh, really? If the thought of being around me bothers you that much then let me make this easy on you."

He leaned in. "Frankie."

She held out her hand. "No, please allow me to

finish. You were Mr. Nice guy while we were Kayaking, and kissing, and having your way. But the minute I take some time to myself to digest everything, then you want to act like you can't be around me?"

"Frankie."

Closing her eyes, she continued. "And, you know what? To think I was actually considering calling you, to discuss taking things slow and seeing where it goes. Hmm," she groaned.

"I would love that."

She did a double-take. "What?"

"I said, I would love that. That's actually why I came over here. I begged Bree for your address so I could talk to you first thing. I even told Grant — I'll do him this one favor by taking the case and seeing it through to the end. But afterward, I'd have to sever all ties with the resort. That way I could officially date the director of HR without it being a conflict of interest."

The corners of Frankie's mouth slowly began to curl upward. "You said that to Grant?"

"Yes, ma'am. I meant every word I said to you earlier, Frankie. Now, you can take all the time you need to think about us and pray about making the best decision. It's not like we don't have time on our hands with this pending case. But, when all is said and done, I'm going to pursue you. My only hope is that my pursuit will be well received."

Frankie's gaze eased downward, feeling foolish

for picking an argument with him. Again, it was the walls of defense that emerged, every single time. In reality, what she really desired was another chance and he was giving it to her. All she had to do was respond.

"Are you going to say anything? Or are you just going to leave me standing here looking like a fool." He smiled.

Just beyond where he stood, she could hear the birds singing a beautiful melody. She could see the flowers that looked a little brighter, and she could feel the tropical breeze that flowed a little different this morning.

"You don't look like a fool. At least not to me. I'm the one standing here with crazy hair," she said, lifting a strand.

He inched closer. "Mmm. That's a matter of opinion. Your hair looks perfect to me. And, so does everything else about you, even down to your pink toenail polish. If I wasn't on temporary hire, I'd hold you close to me and kiss those perfect lips of yours, but I guess for now I have to tame myself."

Frankie motioned toward her lips with a finger. "Mmm. Not a good idea anyway. I have the whole morning breath thing going on and you know how that can be."

David burst into laughter. "Woman, that never stopped me before."

Chapter 16

Meg

By the weekend, the newness of Meg's engagement ring still hadn't settled in. The obsession to look at it, and hold it up in the mirror had become a thing. But she didn't care. It would be a long time before the gem wrapped around her finger would feel familiar.

On the other hand, something else that didn't feel familiar was Mr. Fennley's presence, back at the B&B again.

Meg found the Fennley's on the back deck eating breakfast together. "Now, this is what I like to see. How are you two doing on this lovely Saturday morning?"

Portia Fennley smiled. "We couldn't be better. Isn't that right, Honey."

He nodded. "I'm glad to be back, Miss Carter."

He placed his hand over Portia's. "Not only because I missed my beautiful wife, but because the atmosphere over here is heavenly compared to The Cove. Don't get me wrong, it's a beautiful resort, but nothing compares to this peaceful experience that we're having here at the B&B. Isn't that right, babe?"

"It sure is."

Portia signaled to her husband. "Would you mind grabbing a bagel and another coffee refill for us? I might as well make sure I'm good and full before we head down to the beach."

Meg waved them off. "Please, stay put. I can grab that for you."

Mr. Fennley chuckled. "Anybody who knows my wife, knows how particular she is about her bagels. She spreads one half with cream cheese, the other with jelly, then mushes the two together just so for a match made in heaven. You and Parker have already done so much for us, why don't you stay out here and enjoy the view?"

"Are you sure?" Meg asked.

"I'm certain."

After he left, she wasn't quite sure what to say. Could she talk about their awkward encounter the other day? No. Even though the thought did cross her mind. Instead, she figured the safest thing to do was boast about the island.

"Not sure what you guys have planned after the beach, but uh, there's lots to see and do around here.

You could go deep sea fishing, take a tour via golf cart through Dunmore town, or even take a sunset cruise. Your choices are endless," she said.

The serious look smeared across her face appeared distracted. "Thanks, Meg. I appreciate it, I really do. But, there's something more pressing that I wanted to discuss with you."

Good grief. If only this woman could be like the rest of the guests, peacefully relaxing, soaking up the atmosphere and enjoying life instead of trying to make hers miserable.

She folded her arms, wearing a disguised look as she wore her Jackie O. sunglasses and wide brimmed beach hat. "I owe you an apology. A sincere apology. A completely transparent apology, unlike the first one I gave you." She took a breath. "From one woman to another, I'm sorry for being such a distraction around here and for not respecting the boundaries between you and Parker."

Interesting.

"Not that it should matter, but by the time we arrived, I had my mind made up that I was divorcing my husband as soon as we caught the next flight headed back home."

"Mrs. Fennley, really, I'm thankful for the acknowledgement, but you don't have to explain."

"Please call me Portia, and I want to explain. I need to get it off my chest."

"Okay — Portia."

"Like I was saying. I had my mind made up. And, from the moment I descended down the stairwell to the basement, Parker was the first man I saw — an easy pawn to help make my husband jealous. And, since he introduced you as his manager. Well, I guess I ran with it, viewing him as a way to strike a chord. Stupid, I know. But, that's what I did. Of course, when you behave like that all it does is backfire in the end, which is exactly what happened. I feel foolish for having to admit this to you. But it's the truth, and I hope you will forgive me."

In Meg's mind this was an unexpected twist to breakfast hour at Seaside. But, in her lifetime she'd seen and heard worse, so she just nodded along. Actually, she'd even giggled to herself as she thought of starting a new guest experience journal. She'd stolen the journal idea from her past stays at cabins and B&B's, where folks wrote a journal entry about their stay. It would be the perfect tradition to add to Seaside B&B. Except for Portia's entry, what could she write? Details of the many ways she tried to seduce the owner. No! Of course not. Meg would never display such a thing for public consumption, but that didn't stop her from thinking it.

"Portia, we all go through rough patches. Parker and I just recently went through one, ourselves. I'm sure we were presenting ourselves more like platonic co-workers more than anything else. It's not entirely your fault."

Portia continued staring out toward the water. "I'm a married woman. It shouldn't matter. For now, we've laid our differences aside, but when we get back home we plan to seek out marital counseling," she explained, then turned towards Meg. Sliding her glasses down.

"I heard that congratulations are in order. The two of you are engaged." She smiled.

"Yes, we are. After smoothing out a few things, we realized that it's only right. It's time," Meg replied.

"That's wonderful. I'm happy for you. For me, getting engaged was one of the happiest times in my life. But, if I could go back in time and give advice to my old self, there's one important thing I would tell her."

Feeling cautious Meg asked, "What's that?"

"I would tell her to spend more time planning for the marriage than for the wedding. The ring, the parties, the gifts — it's all exciting. But planning for a lifetime together. That, my dear, is the challenge." She slid her glasses back on. "But, coming here to this island, and having time to clear our minds together, so we can get back to the basics. Hopefully, it will be a form of healing for us. That coupled with therapy."

Meg looked across the ocean, then closed her eyes, inhaling the breeze. "It is a beautiful place. Something about the atmosphere is healing to the soul. Maybe it's all the vitamin D, I'm not sure."

"Well, you guys live here twenty-four-seven. So,

take advantage of it. Don't make your entire lives about work with no joy, and rest and relaxation infused in there," Portia expressed.

"My sentiments exactly."

The conversation was interrupted by Mr. Fennley carrying a full tray of delectable treats, coupled with his wife's favorite bagel combination. "Here you are, Dear. I brought extras for the road just in case."

Meg winked at Portia, appreciating their candid moment together. "I'm going to let you two get back to enjoying this wonderful view in peace. If there's anything you need, you know where to find me."

* * *

"I have a recommendation for the housekeeping position," Meg implied, sliding the resume across his desk.

He picked up the piece of paper, and began reading aloud. "Anita Brown. Ten years of experience at a hotel. Five years prior experience working at a commercial property. How did her references pan out?"

"Everyone spoke highly of her. I don't know what it is, but there's something about her that just feels cozy."

Parker chuckled. "Cozy? It sounds like you're referencing a blanket more than a housekeeper."

He was right. It was the perfect description for a blanket, but Anita made her feel that way too. She had the look of a young grandmother, an endearing smile, and a gentleness about her that Meg thought the guests might appreciate.

"Just wait until you meet her for yourself. She agreed to have a meet and greet with you. I figured you could give her a tour around the B&B, give her an idea of what you're looking for, and get a feel for her yourself. If you don't walk about with the cozy, sweet grandma vibes then I'd be shocked."

She watched as he placed the resume down, and walked around the desk, beckoning for her affection.

"If you like her, then I trust your judgment. The only thing that matters to me is that you're happy. That we're happy."

The sweet taste of his lips gently drawing her closer was what captivated her most. Also, his willingness to acknowledge what was most important. Her partner was finally back — mentally and emotionally, which is all she ever wanted.

A knock on the door brought their time for affection to an abrupt halt. "Look at you two love birds. The engagement stage has elevated you to an all-new level of sappiness, hasn't it?" Savannah said, teasing them.

Throwing her arms open wide, Meg shouted. "Where have you been? There's a whole renovation project by the name of Seaside B&B, just sitting here waiting for your level of design expertise."

Savannah squeezed Meg, then her brother before explaining. "I'm just waiting for this guy to get on the good foot." She looked around. "This house is in great shape. It doesn't look like it needs much at all."

Parker nodded. "It doesn't. However, when you see the second house, I'm sure you'll change your opinion. I'm setting up a meeting with Miguel, as early as next week. I'm sure he'll show up with a hammer in hand, ready to get to work."

Savannah placed both hands in the praying position. "That sounds amazing. But, that's not why I stopped by today."

Sensing more of a serious tone, Meg glanced at Parker. She always had a fun-loving relationship with his sister, right from the start. Even his mother and youngest sister, Alyssa. They were a warm family — kind and supportive. They'd bend over backwards to do anything for their beloved Parker and would do the same for anyone who loved him.

"Do I sense a pregnancy announcement coming on?" Meg smiled.

She laughed. "Oh, no. My hands are full with the two I have now. Good gracious, no."

Well, then what's on your mind?" Parker asked.

Savannah began pacing around the room. "You can freely come out and tell me if you absolutely hate the idea, but I was wondering if you two would ever consider getting married right here at the B&B?"

He squinted, looking at Meg. But before he could comment, Savannah continued further. "Here me out. I had a dream about this. One I could see as clear as day. I could design an arch for you. One that fits your style and blends in lovely with the look of the property. You could close down the place for the weekend or maybe an evening, making it an intimate event with all those you desire to be in attendance."

Both listened in silence, but internally Meg was warming up to the idea. After all, it was the place where Parker proposed. And, it definitely was the same place where Barnes and his wife carried out their legacy of love.

"Keep going," Meg said.

With energy bubbling over, Savannah spread her hands wide, envisioning the scene. "Can't you just see it? You could exchange your vows down by the water. You could set up white tents and a dance floor closer to the house with gorgeous flowers overflowing everywhere. This place provides the perfect ambiance for a romantic beach wedding. But this would have to be an idea that you truly wanted for yourselves. I'm just the messenger, sent here after having a dream." She chuckled.

All it took was one confirming look from Parker and they were sold. It was certainly an unexpected idea, but a welcomed one.

"There's just one more thing," Savannah said.

Meg frowned. "Uh-oh. Here it comes."

"No uh-ohs. I promise this is a good thing. After waking up from my dream I couldn't help but do a little research on the B&B, dating back to when it opened. Were you two aware that Barnes and his wife, Evelyn, hosted an opening ceremony and invited a pastor to cut the ribbon and pray a blessing over the place?"

Parker hesitated, looking at Meg. "No. He never mentioned anything about it."

"Well, that makes sense given that it was so long ago. But, check this out. I looked him up, and it turns out the same pastor resides at a sweet little chapel in the community. It might be worth your while to go meet him. At the least, maybe he could give you a little history about the B&B. And at best —"

Meg felt a surge of excitement take over. She could see exactly where Savannah was going with this and thought it was a pretty brilliant idea. "At best we could hit it off with him and ask him to officiate over our ceremony, right here at Seaside."

Savannah raised her hand. "High five, girl. See there. I know it's kind of cliché, but great minds really do think alike."

Meg smiled. "They do. Honestly, I love the idea if we could pull it off. Parker, what do you think?"

Silence fell over the room as Parker scratched his chin. He took what seemed like an eternity to arrive at a final conclusion. "I think it's a lovely idea. A romantic one, actually. But — I'll only agree to it under one condition."

Savannah looked at Meg, and Meg looked right back at her. It was usually the men who cared less about the details. All they usually wanted was for their lady to be happy.

"Okayyy," Meg said. "Well, don't hold us in suspense. What's the condition?"

"Marry me next weekend. Let's semi elope, throwing all the stress of wedding planning behind us. We already have the venue, and we have each other. What do you say?"

Meg reared her head back. "You can't be serious?"

"Oh, but I am. I already told you earlier. You mean the world to me, and there's nothing that could ever stand in the way of me wanting to spend forever with you. So — Meg Carter. Will you marry me next weekend?"

Meg's dimples spoke volumes as she leapt into the arms of her man. She'd never spoken about it, but the idea of bypassing all the fancy foo foo wedding plans thrilled her. It was never her thing to begin with. She was only willing to go along with it when she was engaged to John because it was what his family expected of them.

She paused. "I love the idea. But my Dad and

stepmom would be so heartbroken if they couldn't attend."

"So, how about we exchange our intimate vows, then at a date that's convenient for everyone, throw something larger here at the B&B?"

Meg cupped her palms around his cheeks. "Parker Wilson. Have I ever told you how amazing you are?" she said, then planted the biggest kiss, not just once, but several times all over his lips.

That afternoon, Savannah eased out the door, just as quickly as she'd eased in. It had been one of their best visits in a long time. One that would change the path to their future, forever.

Chapter 17

Frankie

Three months later — Frankie stood in the archway, listening as the realtor congratulated David on his new home. The home had all the perks of a waterfront property. It sat on almost an acre across the street from the Caribbean Sea, boasting three bedrooms, a chef's kitchen, and a view to die for. It would be his personal oasis and she couldn't be happier for him. And, with the victory of the resort's lawsuit behind him, David was now free to live and do as he pleased.

After he escorted the realtor out, Frankie applauded and handed over a gift bag. "Congrats to the new homeowner. Living out of a hotel has its perks, but I'm sure it feels nice to call this place home." She smiled.

"It does have a special ring to it." Sifting through the tissue paper he said, "Ah, a bottle of wine. Thank you. You'll have to crack it open with me so we can celebrate." He chuckled. "As for the house, I certainly couldn't have done it without your help. And, yes, there's definitely something about this place that feels much more — permanent compared to a hotel."

As he spoke, she pulled two glasses and a wine opener out of her bag. "I always like to be prepared."

"That makes two of us," David said. "As much as I love this house, it's definitely going to take some getting used to. Living alone will definitely come with its challenges," he explained, sliding his fingers between hers while gently leading her to the veranda.

"What's there to get used to? Listening to the soothing sound of the Caribbean Sea? Heaven forbid you'd have to adjust to such a noise," she teased.

The home and the view were a far cry from what she was accustomed to on her side of the island. Although, Frankie was always cozy living in her humble abode. It might feel a little different when her roommate moved out. But she'd adjust and still enjoy long walks up to the coast.

He continued. "Well, let's see. You have the ferocious sound of the water, the gorgeous sunsets, and those breathtaking sunrises to contend with. Good gracious, how is a man to handle all that on his own?"

Giving him the side eye, Frankie said, "Okay,

now you're just bragging. Most people I know would die to have those kinds of issues. I really think you'll be okay."

When he pulled the sliding glass door open, his eyes skimmed the property and beyond. "I don't know, Frankie. I believe there's a whole lot of truth to the saying about man — and how he was not created to live life alone. It would be an awful shame for all this square footage to go to waste, without having you here with me, by my side."

It felt like her heart dropped, triggering all kinds of feelings in the pit of her stomach. She'd walked right into that one, blindly, and all she could seem to offer in return was crickets.

He grabbed both of her hands. "Do you remember what I told you right before I took the case?"

She shook her head no.

"I specifically told you that I planned to pursue you." He then eased down to his knee as he reached for his back pocket. "And, my only hope was that my pursuit was well received."

Oh, my dear Lord in heaven. He's about to propose.

He cleared his throat. "You don't have to respond today, Frankie. Maybe you'll need more time and if you do, I'll completely understand. But I want to present this ring to you. It represents the vow I made to myself and I'm making to you to finish what we started."

He removed from the box the same ring he'd presented years ago. Except this time there was something that he pointed out. "On the inside there's an inscription that reads, forever. The same way I held on to this ring, is the same way I want to hold on to you — forever. Frankie Marie Jones, it is my hope that you'll consider having me as your lawfully wedded husband, forever. I knew from the minute I laid eyes on you, again, that I wanted you forever, but it's not solely about what I want. It's about what you want as well. Will you marry me?"

It felt like a weight had been lifted. A deep sense of relief from all the past pain, drama, wrong decision-making, and old wounds began to ease off her body. It's not that David possessed a magical cure by any stretch of the imagination. There was no such thing as a magical cure. But finally, she was standing before her person. The man she was destined to be with, and somehow that made this moment feel right.

"Forever, as in till death do us part? As in, you actually want to sign up to deal with my crazy butt for the rest of your life?" She giggled.

David nodded. "Yes, that's the kind of forever I'm talking about. What do you say?"

A tear slid down her cheek. "Yes, I'll marry you — forever."

* * *

It didn't take many visits to book club night to realize its true purpose. Frankie and Meg read the various books, and mingled with the group. But the physical act of gathering to discuss books relating to relationships and women's topics made it so much more fulfilling. Plus, it helped foster their friendship. It created a place with a little time away from the guys, and a space where self-expression was openly welcomed, and not judged. Therefore, the last session of the month with the same group of women would be no different. In their eyes, it may have even been a time for healing.

"So, it turns out the main character wasn't a cheater after all? Who knew!" one of the participants chimed in.

Another contributed. "I knew it right from the start. At times our society can be so quick to assume the worst, but there are other things people struggle with besides infidelity."

Frankie nodded. "Yeah, and in this case, it was just like you mentioned. He'd learned how to be affectionate behind closed doors, but that was about it."

Meg agreed. "And, to assume your partner will automatically understand how you feel, or somehow know everything you're thinking without you communicating — well I can speak personally when I say that's just a recipe for disaster."

The women nodded along before moving on to

the concluding pages. That's when Meg leaned in, stirring up their usual side conversation.

"Okay, so a little off topic, but I was wondering if you and David decided on a date yet?"

Frankie threw a dagger back at Meg with her eyes. "Don't you think I should be asking you the same question? I'm still trying to figure out why you guys didn't just carry out your plans of getting married right away and throwing a larger shindig later. Do you know how many women would die to have their ceremony at the B&B? The property is stunning to say the least."

In a sing-song way, Meg replied, "I know, I know. And, it will still be there when we're ready. Savannah had an amazing idea for us to get married there. I have to give her the credit, but there's something to be said about deciding to wait a few months to give family and friends back home time to join us."

Adjusting her shawl, Frankie said, "True. It will be more special for you that way, that's for sure. I, on the other hand, don't have many to invite. So, something small, breathtaking, and low-key like the B&B would be perfect for me."

Wearing the biggest grin, Meg leaned over and whispered. "That's kind of what I've been wanting to talk to you about. Parker and I were wondering how you and David would feel about getting married at Seaside, house #2? As you know, we're planning on having our wedding at the current beach house. But we were thinking about testing the waters with hosting weddings at the second property. I can't think of a better wedding to start with than the wedding of one of my best friends," she said, nudging Frankie. "It wouldn't be ready for another six months or so. But we'd create a digital prototype of the anticipated finished look. And, we wouldn't charge you anything. All we'd ask is that you allow us to use some of your photos for marketing future events. That's only if you and David were comfortable with the idea."

With a nudge back, Frankie squealed. "Are you serious?"

By now the women in the group must've grown used to their shenanigans. No one looked up or turned around. It was almost as if they were oblivious to Frankie's high-pitched voice.

"I don't know what to say," Frankie expressed, holding her face.

"Just say yes!" Meg laughed. "Frankie, I don't know if you realize it or not, but we've come so far together. I remember the first day I met you like it was yesterday. You drove me around the grounds of The Cove in a golf cart, welcoming me on board as a new member of the staff. Then you invited me to become your housemate when I barely knew where I was going or what I was doing with my life. That kind of friendship is hard to come by. So, if there's anything I can do to aid in your happily ever after, then I'm all in."

Frankie hugged her friend's arm. "And, I'd do it for you all over again if I could," she whispered. "How about this? For now, let's finish up our book, and tonight when we get together with the guys, I'll mention it to David."

Meg winked. "Sounds good."

* * *

"A candlelit dinner on Harbor Island for four. Life just doesn't get any better than this," Frankie announced, reaching for her glass.

"Oh, yes it does," Parker replied. "I'd like to propose a toast."

Meg, Parker, Frankie and David sat surrounded by flaming torches at Seaside B&B. A few guests, including Ms. Beekman, lingered at the other tables, while Chef Sean happily served them.

"This toast is for many things including the great company among us this evening, the new friendship being formed between myself and David, and to our beautiful brides to be. David, I'm almost certain you share my sentiments when I say we are the two luckiest men in the world."

David held up his glass. "I agree wholeheartedly. And might I add a specific toast to you and Meg for extending a beautiful place for us to have our wedding. We can't thank you enough."

The sound of clanking glasses left Frankie with a feeling bubbling on the inside of her. For a change, it felt like everything had come full circle, working out exactly how life intended it to be."

As everyone settled down, Meg slumped back in her chair. "Man, oh man. It's been one heck of a year. To think around this time last year, Parker and I were meeting at what I considered to be my glamorous beach rental that I found online. Boy, did that turn out to be a bust. And, you Frankie had no idea that David was back in New York preparing to make a grand reemergence back into your life."

Frankie's eyes widened. "Can you imagine if we had the ability to know these things in advance? I could've saved myself a bunch of drama and claimed back wasted time."

"Sorry, no can do," David replied. "It's the hard times that teach us the best life lessons. You can't avoid it, you just have to go through it."

Frankie winked. "Spoken like a true wise man."

Parker nodded along, as he reached for Meg's hand. "The question is — where do we all go from here? Where do we see ourselves ten, fifteen, maybe even twenty years from now? We're all on the brink of marriage, for all of us it's a second chance at love. David is successfully practicing law. Frankie, you're at the top of your game as the director of HR. And,

Meg, you and I have gotten off to a phenomenal start here at Seaside with plans for great things to come. But all the accolades and accomplishments mean absolutely nothing if we don't have each other."

While affectionately massaging Parker's arm, Meg replied, "You know what, Babe, that's a great question. We make plans for so many things that have to do with success, and climbing that ladder, but how often do we think to stop and make plans for our relationships and our personal lives?"

Frankie reached for the bottle on ice and began filling everyone's glass again. "I do believe we have cause for another toast. If everyone will grab their glasses."

Frankie wasn't big on speeches, but she knew this one would flow seamlessly from the heart. "Reuniting with David has simplified a lot of things about love for me. In my book, love doesn't have to be overly complicated like it had been in my past. Love has to be showered in patience, or else it won't stand a chance. Love should always be backed with honesty, and should involve a whole lot of forgiveness. Finally, love puts each other first and vows to have fun living life together. Period." She raised her glass. "And with that in mind, I'd like to propose a final toast in honor of our ten-to-fifteen-year plan — actually in honor of our forever plan. May our future be packed with all the ingredients I just mentioned. Love, honesty, forgiveness, patience, and a whole lot of fun. Any plan short of these things, just won't do."

A final clanking of the glasses under the tropical moonlight solidified their plans and more importantly, their bond.

New Tropical Breeze Series!

Can she find love when she's healing from heartache?

After a painful end to a long engagement, all Meg wants out of life is a fresh start.

She can't think of a better way to begin than by advancing her career in the hotel industry. When an opportunity comes along to accept a position at a five-star resort, she secures a beach house, packs her bags, and heads to the Bahamas.

But her oasis has been sold in an auction and the new owner and heartthrob, Parker Wilson, has no intention of holding onto a contract.

She'll have nowhere to stay, nowhere to heal, nowhere to grow if she gives in to his flippant attitude about her future.

When Meg digs her heels in and refuses to leave, will this drive them further into the arena of enemies? Or will they find common ground and potentially become lovers?

Tropical Encounter is a clean beach read with a splash of romance that's sure to give you all the feels.

Pull up your favorite beach chair and watch as Meg and Parker's story unfolds!

Tropical Breeze Series:
   Tropical Encounter: Book 1
   Tropical Escape: Book 2

Tropical Moonlight: Book 3
Tropical Summer: Book 4
Tropical B&B: Book 5
Tropical Christmas: Book 6

Solomons Island Series

She's single, out of a job, and has a week to decide what to do with her life.

He lost his fiancé to a fatal accident while serving in the coast guard.

Will a chance encounter lead Clara and Mike to find love?

Clara's boss, Joan Russell, was a wealthy owner of a beachfront mansion, who recently passed away.

Joan's estranged family members have stepped in, eager to collect their inheritance and dismiss Clara of her duties.

With the clock winding down, will Clara find a job and make a new life for herself on Solomons Island? Will a chance encounter with Mike lead her to meet the man of her dreams? Or will Clara have to do the unthinkable and return home to a family who barely cares for her existence?

This women's divorce fiction book will definitely leave you wanting more! If you love women's fiction and clean romance, this series is for you. Embark on a journey of new beginnings and pick up your copy today!

<u>Solomons Island Series:</u>

Beachfront Inheritance: Book 1

Beachfront Promises: Book 2

Beachfront Embrace: Book 3

Beachfront Christmas: Book 4

Beachfront Memories: Book 5

Beachfront Secrets: Book 6

Pelican Beach Series

She's recently divorced. He's a widower. Will a chance encounter lead to true love?

If you like sweet romance about second chances then you'll love The Inn At Pelican Beach!

At the Inn, life is filled with the unexpected. Payton is left to pick up the pieces after her divorce is finalized. Seeking a fresh start, she returns to her home town in Pelican Beach.

Determined to move on with her life, she finds herself caught up in the family business at The Inn. It may not be her passion, but anything is better than what her broken marriage had to offer. Payton doesn't wallow in her sorrows long before her opportunity at a second chance shows up. Is there room in her heart to love again? She'll soon find out!

In this first book of the Pelican Beach series, passion, renewed strength, and even a little sibling rivalry are just a few of the emotions that come to mind.

Visit The Inn and walk hand in hand with Payton as she heals and seeks to restore true love.

Get your copy of this clean romantic beach read today!

Pelican Beach Series:
   The Inn at Pelican Beach: Book 1
   Sunsets at Pelican Beach: Book 2
   A Pelican Beach Affair: Book 3
   Christmas at Pelican Beach: Book 4
   Sunrise At Pelican Beach: Book 5

www.ingramcontent.com/pod-product-compliance
Lightning Source LLC
Chambersburg PA
CBHW070502200726
48293CB00007B/2339